Dangerous Desires

"Fires and floods, muggings and lost kids." Phoebe shuddered. She had awakened in a great mood, but the news reports in the paper and on TV had demolished it. Natural disaster and human malevolence waged a relentless war against the helpless. At least the Charmed Ones could fight the demonic evil they encountered.

"Are you okay?" Concerned, Piper rested a hand on Phoebe's knee.

"Yeah, it's just that—I wish my visions weren't so selective because then we could keep more of this awful stuff from happening."

Phoebe's stomach suddenly heaved with nausea, and a rush of dizziness made her head spin. Her coffee mug slipped from her hand as she gasped and doubled over.

"Phoebe!" Piper threw her arms around her stricken sister and let the mug land on the carpet.

"What is it?" Prue jumped from her chair and knelt down by the sofa. "A vision?"

Charmed®

Published by Simon & Schuster

BEWARE WHAT YOU WISH

An original novel by Diana G. Gallagher
Based on the hit TV series
created by Constance M. Burge

SIMON SPOTLIGHT ENTERTAINMENT
New York   London   Toronto   Sydney

First Simon Spotlight Entertainment edition May 2005
First Simon Pulse edition May 2002
First Pocket Pulse edition August 2001
® & © 2001 Spelling Television Inc. All Rights Reserved.

S|S|E

SIMON SPOTLIGHT ENTERTAINMENT
An imprint of Simon & Schuster Children's Publishing Division
1230 Avenue of the Americas, New York, New York 10020

Manufactured in the United States of America

10 9 8 7

ISBN-13: 978-0-7434-1238-4
ISBN-10: 0-7434-1238-9

With affection for
Theresa D'Andrea

BEWARE WHAT YOU WISH

CHAPTER
1

Startling, dark eyes caught Prue Halliwell off guard as she stepped through heavy wooden doors into a foyer lit by flickering wall sconces. This was not what she had expected when Stephen Tremaine's housekeeper had directed her into the library to wait.

Her sister Piper's warning over breakfast that morning rushed to mind. "Be careful, Prue. I've heard that guy is tougher than a stale cookie and incredibly vain."

"Vain with good reason," Phoebe, the youngest of the three sisters, had added. "According to the gossip columnists Mr. Tremaine is *the* most sought after bachelor in town."

"Being one of the *richest* bachelors in the state may have something to do with that." Piper had

1

patted Prue's shoulder with sympathy. "Vain is the operative word, Prue. Better make darn sure you get the lighting right."

Now Prue's hand tightened on her camera strap as she watched artificial torchlight play across the primitive visage before her. Set in parched, brown hide and ringed in white, the lifeless eye sockets stared back with a defiance untouched by time.

The primitive mask was a unique reminder to all that Stephen Tremaine was in complete control, Prue realized uneasily.

"Make sure you get the lighting *perfect*," Phoebe had added earlier that morning. "Tremaine has a business reputation as a shark."

Prue did not take her sisters' warnings lightly. The wealthy entrepreneur she had been sent to photograph was rumored to have an ego that matched his bulging Wall Street portfolio. If Tremaine found her work less than flattering and complained to the editor of *415* magazine, the consequences could put a serious dent in her puny-by-comparison bank account.

"Do you find it disturbing?" a man asked from behind her.

"Not particularly, no." Prue glanced back as Stephen Tremaine closed the library door.

Forty-three, with closely cropped salt-and-pepper hair that emphasized the severity of his angular face, Tremaine had a more commanding presence than Prue had anticipated. Casual gray slacks and a blue blazer worn over a white turtleneck softened his austere expression without diluting his confident demeanor. As Phoebe had observed, he was attractive if you liked brainy GI Joe types.

And driven by ambition, Prue reminded herself. Twenty years ago Tremaine had created and sold computer gaming software from an efficiency apartment in Oakland. As his company had grown into an industry giant, he had expanded into military simulations and applications. Last year he had sold Tremaine Enterprises for millions.

Now Tremaine was running for Congress, which was why she had been assigned to photograph him. The photo would be published along with an interview in *415*.

"An intriguing response." Tremaine hesitated, looking surprised, then smiled as he moved toward Prue. "Most women find my collection repulsive."

"Do they?" Caught off guard by the intensity of Tremaine's gray gaze, Prue turned back to the mask.

Perched on a pedestal, the artifact dominated the library foyer. The oval mask was fringed in partially beaded strands of coarse, black hair. Colorful pigments crisscrossed the face, separating the eyes from a gaping mouth inlaid with discolored, broken teeth. Human teeth, if Prue wasn't mistaken.

"West African, isn't it?" Prue asked with that slight, self-satisfied smile Piper called her gotcha grin.

Tremaine cocked an eyebrow, taken aback again. Apparently, none of the women he knew were familiar with cultural antiquities. "Yes, a spirit mask from the Congo Basin."

Prue extended her hand and introduced herself.

"I'm more delighted than you can imagine, Ms. Halliwell." Tremaine gripped Prue's hand in both of his. "It's not often I meet someone who appreciates the ancient crafts."

More appreciative of the ancient Craft than you'll ever know, Prue thought. She and her two sisters were the Charmed Ones, witches endowed with supernatural powers and an unquestioned obligation to defend the innocent against evil. Since they had all moved back to the Victorian house they had inherited from their grandmother and discovered *The Book of Shadows,* their powers and the bond between them had grown stronger.

"Especially someone so beautiful." Tremaine held Prue's wary gaze as he released her hand. When she didn't respond immediately, he cleared his throat and self-consciously averted his eyes.

Prue couldn't tell if the candidate was being sincere or simply angling for her vote. She didn't agree with his politics, which was bad if he wanted a date, but irrelevant regarding her job. She smiled to smooth over the awkward moment and raised her camera. "Shall we?"

"First, let me show you some of my other prized pieces." Tremaine put his hand on Prue's back and gently urged her toward the expansive library beyond the foyer.

Prue's indignation at Tremaine's possessive manner was forgotten as she stepped into his magnificent library. Thousands of books, many of them leather-bound editions, lined floor-to-ceiling shelving on three walls. Three tall arched windows and French doors leading into a garden were set into the fourth wall. A variety of masks, tapestries, leather shields, and Native American dream catchers hung on mahogany-paneled wall space between the bookshelves. Other cases with glass doors contained carved totems, pottery, jewelry, tools, and idols fashioned from metal, stone, and wood.

The stunning sight took Prue's breath away.

"You're impressed," Tremaine said, smiling.

"Yes, I am," Prue answered honestly, disarmed by the man's almost boyish delight with her reaction. She nodded as her educated gaze swept over the room. Many of the artifacts had easily recognizable origins—intricate Chinese carvings in jade, Egyptian mosaics, and Aztec sun stones—while others eluded her expertise. She bent forward to study an oil pot etched with the figure of Zeus, wondering how such an exquisite ancient piece had ended up in Tremaine's private collection instead of a museum.

"Care to guess?" Tremaine asked.

"Greek. Fourth or fifth century B.C." Prue straightened, being careful not to let on that she was disturbed. She had done business with every major art and antiquity collector in San Francisco when she had worked at Buckland's auction house— except for Stephen Tremaine. Exactly *how* had he acquired so many priceless artifacts?

"Fifth," Tremaine said. "It was found in a dig I financed five years ago near the site of ancient Delphi."

Prue didn't ask if he had used theft or bribery to remove an oil-burning urn from Greece. It was highly unlikely the Greek government had willingly let such a rare, almost perfectly preserved artifact leave the country.

"There's no other quite like it in the entire world." Tremaine stared into the case as he spoke.

Prue wasn't sure if the candidate was overcome with awe for the history behind the piece and respect for the hands that had created it or simply consumed by pride and the thrill of possessing the unique. Or elements of both, she thought. A man with Tremaine's abilities and aspirations would be more complex than his public profile. She had expected him to be arrogant and demanding. Instead, he had been gracious and charming. She had no idea which persona defined the real Stephen Tremaine. Playing it safe, she shifted gears before she said something she'd regret.

"I need to get these shots while the light is right, Mr. Tremaine." Prue glanced at the sunlight streaming through the windows, which would give her sufficient back lighting. One of the filtered lenses in her bag would soften the hard lines of his face. She hoped the marvels of modern technology would create the illusion of youthful dignity that Mr. Tremaine required.

"Of course." Tremaine nodded curtly, then turned and strode across the room. He sighed as he leaned against his desk. "I suppose you want the usual head shot."

"Actually, I was thinking of something a little more creative," Prue said. Actually, she was thinking on her feet. In the event Tremaine managed to get elected, it couldn't hurt to have a congressman as a happy customer. "A shot that says something about the man behind the public persona."

"Such as?" Tremaine asked.

Prue dropped her bag on the sofa and talked as she fished for the filtered lens. "Upper body shot in front of a display case holding one of these fabulous pieces. You pick."

"Excellent idea." Suddenly enthused, Tremaine withdrew a key from his jacket pocket and unlocked the nearest display case. "Will there be a caption under the picture?"

"Most likely." Prue smiled her gotcha smile. Diplomacy when properly applied packed a powerful punch. Tremaine may or may not have been playing her for a fool with his compliments, but she was in complete control now.

"What is that?" Prue asked as Tremaine pulled a crudely carved stone statue from the case. Egg-shaped and roughly eight inches tall with barely discernible facial and body features, it seemed an odd choice compared to Tremaine's more elaborate treasures.

"My experts believe it's a spirit stone." Tremaine cupped the statue in both hands, his gaze trained on it with unguarded admiration.

"Go on." Prue snapped off a series of shots from slightly different angles.

"The evidence suggests it's from an obscure tribe that inhabited the central Amazon regions of South America roughly three thousand years ago," Tremaine continued.

Prue captured his satisfied grin on film and kept shooting. "Fascinating."

"Yes, quite." Tremaine's face clouded. "However, my knowledge and appreciation of ancient cultures won't help me defeat my opponent."

"Probably not," Prue agreed. Noel Jefferson was the other contender for a recently vacated congressional seat in San Francisco. Younger and better looking, the idealistic public defender was leading in the polls in spite of Tremaine's political connections and money. Dedicated to fighting injustice, Jefferson had already sewn up the Halliwell vote. However, with several weeks to go before the election, Tremaine had a better-than-even chance of catching up with his promises of less government interference and more corporate responsibility. The upwardly mobile, business-oriented half of the electorate loved the successful, no-nonsense rich guy.

Prue continued to shoot as Tremaine's jaw flexed and his grip tightened on the ancient stone.

"You have no idea how much I wish I wasn't running against Noel Jefferson. The man's record is—" Tremaine's eyes closed, and he swayed on his feet as though suddenly overcome with dizziness.

Prue lowered the camera and instinctively reached out. "Are you all right?"

"I'm fine." Tremaine brushed away her hand and her concern. Obviously shaken, he put the primitive stone back in the case with a trembling hand and stammered an excuse. "My schedule's been so full I've skipped one too many meals."

Although it escaped Tremaine's notice, Prue saw that he had set the statue down on the rounded edge of its base. As the wobbling stone started to fall, she concentrated and flicked her finger to move it onto its flattened bottom, saving the glass shelf from cracking. Having turned away, Tremaine didn't notice that, either.

"Are we finished?" Composing himself, Tremaine settled into the leather chair behind his desk and flipped open a laptop.

"Yes." Prue realized the candidate was upset because she had witnessed a vulnerable moment. Since he had already made his medical records public, she knew he wasn't hiding a serious condition. Still, a reporter with less integrity than she had might use the incident for political or professional gain. "I'm sure one of these shots will—"

"Then if you don't mind, I've got work to do." Tremaine averted his gaze and turned on the computer.

Annoyed by the rude dismissal, Prue grabbed her camera bag and headed for the door. On closer inspection of the display cases, she realized that, although Tremaine owned some distinctive pieces from the classic ancient cultures, his collection was predominantly comprised of weapons and other artifacts of war and intimidation from warrior societies.

The connection hit Prue as she turned into the foyer. War and intimidation were an appropriate reflection of Tremaine's methods in business and, perhaps, even in politics. Anyone who wanted to hold elected office had to appear to be gracious and charming even if he wasn't.

She cast a quick glance into the dark eyes of the mask on the pedestal and shuddered as she let herself out. Like anyone whose existence was defined exclusively by money and power, maybe Tremaine's life was just as empty as those ancient, lifeless orbs.

CHAPTER 2

Isn't this romantic?" Phoebe grinned as she opened her grandmother's old wicker picnic basket and pulled out a flowered print tablecloth. Her sisters exchanged a glance, as if she had suddenly gone daft.

Wearing a plain cotton T-shirt and a long, casual skirt with sandals, Piper folded her arms, her expression puzzled. "Did you just say 'romantic'?"

"I distinctly heard her say 'romantic.'" Prue, looking chic in hip-hugging jeans and a red halter top, set her camera bag on the picnic table bench and grabbed one end of the tablecloth. Blue eyes framed by shining, shoulder-length black hair twinkled with amusement as she looked pointedly at Piper. "I told you Phoebe wasn't getting out enough."

"True." Piper fought back a smile. "I just never realized weeks of cramming for exams could cause delusions of romance in the romantically deprived."

"Deprived, definitely. Delusional . . . not," Phoebe admitted. The hem of her V-neck blue top rode up as she threw out her arms, exposing a flat stomach as tan as her long, trim legs. "I mean, look at this place!"

Phoebe's gaze swept the expansive city park. The picnic table they had chosen sat atop a grassy rise under the branches of a large oak. Ducks and swans swam in a sun-drenched pond that sparkled in the midst of meadow green below. Elderly people sat on park benches, enjoying the warm afternoon sun or strolled with small dogs. Runners and teenagers on in-line skates and skateboards raced along paths that meandered through thick stands of hardwoods and evergreen trees. Children shouted and laughed in a playground area equipped with wooden climbing scaffolds, slides, and swings. A birthday party, complete with rented pony, overflowed a covered picnic pavilion a hundred yards behind them.

Phoebe breathed in deeply and exhaled slowly. Fresh air and the tranquility of ordinary people engaged in ordinary activities was a soothing respite from the constant battle she and her not-so-ordinary sisters waged against evil. Today she intended to enjoy every demon-free moment of their impromptu family outing, including the affectionate teasing.

Piper glanced around the park and shrugged as she looked back at Phoebe. "I don't get it."

"You don't think this is the *perfect* setting for a

romantic, lazy afternoon picnic?" Phoebe was astounded. Of the three of them, Piper was the most down-to-earth, but she was also the only Halliwell sister who was in love.

"Completely perfect." Piper brushed her long, brown hair behind her ear. "Except that we're three women on a picnic with no men."

Phoebe sighed, exasperated. "But if Leo were here—"

"He's not." Piper tilted her head slightly and set her jaw. Her dark eyes clouded.

Phoebe didn't need a body language dictionary to figure out what *that* meant. Leo had been assigned to protect all the Halliwell sisters when they had discovered their powers, but he had won Piper's heart. However, Leo hadn't been around much lately, and she didn't blame Piper for not wanting to talk about playing second fiddle to White Lighter business all the time.

Correction, Phoebe reminded herself. Piper didn't *dare* complain out loud. Since she had fallen for a man who had died during World War II and had then been enlisted as an agent of good by the big guys in heaven, she had to accept the consequences. As luck would have it, romance between White Lighters and the witches they protected was high up on the White Lighter no-no list. However, when Piper's broken heart had threatened to weaken the Power of Three, Leo's bosses had relented—with one condition. Piper and Leo could pursue their forbidden love as long as it didn't interfere with helping a single innocent.

And helping the innocent was a full-time job for all of them, Phoebe mused. Except unlike Leo, she and her sisters never had to orb out to metaphysical planes unknown to hold up their end of the deal.

"And you and I have no prospects, Phoebe," Prue added.

"Huh?" Phoebe blinked.

"Romantic prospects?" Prue clarified.

"Strictly a temporary situation, I'm sure," Phoebe countered. There was a Mr. Right for her out there somewhere, she assured herself. Better to be patient than to fall for the wrong guy and be sorry forever.

"More temporary than you realize, apparently," Piper said. "Especially if you like tall, tan blond guys."

"Been looking into your crystal ball?" Phoebe asked.

"No, just behind the bar at P3." Piper grinned. "Rick Foreman, the new part-time bartender, couldn't take his eyes off you the other night."

Phoebe frowned, thinking back. She had gone to Piper's club to take a break from the books for a couple of hours last Friday, but she didn't recall a new bartender. "Why didn't you say something?"

"Because last weekend you were focused on your exams and didn't need a distraction," Piper explained.

"Right," Phoebe agreed. "I would have been lousy company. Besides, maybe there won't be any sparks when this Rick and I actually meet."

"Sparks would be good." Prue sighed.

"No instant chemistry between you and the wealthy, passably handsome Mr. Tremaine, Prue?" Piper asked as she removed plastic plates and a thermos of lemonade from the basket.

"Not really." Frowning, Prue set out silverware wrapped in napkins like those Piper used at P3.

"Does that mean you're not quite sure?" Phoebe snapped the lid off a container of cold roast chicken, grabbed a leg, and set the container down.

"No, I'm sure." Prue swung her legs under the table and poured lemonade as Piper and Phoebe sat down. "Stephen Tremaine was actually quite pleasant, which isn't unusual for a politician who wants to win an election, except that I don't agree with any of his positions."

"For business and against the environment among other things," Phoebe said. There was no way she'd ever vote for a millionaire entrepreneur who thought corporations could and should police themselves regarding pollution.

Piper nodded. "But a lot of my customers agree with Tremaine on those issues."

"Apparently, a lot of people agree with your customers, but the real turnoff for me was his—" Prue interrupted herself to take a drink.

"What?" Phoebe paused with a spoonful of potato salad poised in midair. "Bad breath? He cracks his knuckles? Smacks his lips when he eats?"

"Creepy collection." Prue shuddered.

Piper reacted with a start. "Collection of what? Skewered dead bugs? Shrunken heads?"

"Stamps?" Phoebe offered.

"No stamps, but I'd be willing to bet my new cashmere sweater he's got a bug or a head somewhere." Prue smiled. "He's got one of the most impressive collections of artifacts I've ever seen, most of it related to war."

"Are you saying Tremaine is whacko?" Phoebe's eyes narrowed in thought as she nibbled a carrot stick. "That would explain why he's running for Congress. With all his money, he'd have to be nuts to go into politics."

"Not necessarily," Prue said.

"Well, I doubt Stephen Tremaine is motivated by a burning desire to contribute to the common good," Piper said. "The only other reason anyone goes into politics is power."

"That fits Tremaine's personality profile." Prue dropped a chicken bone on her plate and wiped her fingers on a napkin.

Piper's brow furrowed in puzzled contemplation. "I just can't imagine why anyone would want to vote for him."

"He's got a great handshake and a winning smile." Prue shrugged. "That's enough for some people."

"But he's also running a brilliant PR campaign." Phoebe didn't pay much attention to politics as a rule, but Tremaine's hard-hitting message was impossible to ignore. His TV and billboard ads pushing the concept of environmentally friendly industry dominated the airwaves and roadsides. Too many voters couldn't see past the short-term economic gains to consider the long-term potential for envi-

ronmental disaster. Phoebe didn't think it was worth
the risk.

"Well, Tremaine must be a little worried, too,"
Prue said. "Yesterday I actually heard him wish he
wasn't running against Noel Jefferson."

"Now, there's a hunk." Piper grinned. "Not to
mention that he's one of the good guys."

Jefferson, the other wannabe congressman, was a
blondish, brown-eyed, athletic thirty-something
and a dynamic defender of the underprivileged and
unjustly accused. Both candidates were single.

"Mr. Jefferson does have a certain appeal—for a
poor man with principles." Flustered, Phoebe
quickly qualified her observation. "Not that I'm
interested."

"Of course not, but I might be." Prue reached for
the salt and knocked over her glass of lemonade.

Piper's hand shot out to freeze the tipping glass
and the stream of yellow liquid pouring out.

"Piper!" Prue scolded as she set the glass up
right.

"Sorry." Piper winced and unfroze the stream of
lemonade.

Prue grabbed a bunch of paper napkins to wipe
up the spill.

That was a dramatic three seconds, Phoebe
thought, looking around to see if anyone had
noticed. No one had. The grade-school kids playing
kick ball several yards away were focused on their
game, as were their parents. The birthday party
people at the pavilion were busy convincing eager
little pony riders to wait their turn.

"Just my rotten luck 415 sent me to photograph Tremaine." Prue sighed. "At least if I met Noel Jefferson, I could honestly say I intended to vote for him."

"Maybe you'll get your chance next Saturday." Piper set down her fork and patted her stomach. "I'm full."

"What's happening next Saturday?" Phoebe picked up another carrot stick. Piper shot her a scowling glance as she bit off the end. "Am I in trouble?"

"You are if you've forgotten you volunteered to help me with the P3 booth at the Celebrity Charity Bazaar," Piper said.

"Is that this coming Saturday?" Phoebe's big brown eyes widened. She hadn't forgotten her promise. She had just lost track of time because of school.

Piper planned to set up the booth to represent the ambience of P3 with stools, a table or two, non-alcoholic drinks, hot and cold hors d'oeuvres, pictures of the club's interior, and recorded music by the different groups that performed on the P3 stage. The event was being held at the Boardwalk Beach and picnic grounds adjacent to the Gold Coast Amusement Park. Phoebe was looking forward to helping out, especially since a lot of national and local celebrities planned to attend. Who knew where the love of her life might be lurking, waiting to meet a perky witch? Maybe even behind the bar at P3, she thought with a subtle smile.

"You're not going to let me down, are you?" Piper asked.

"My word is my bond." Phoebe solemnly raised her free hand, then popped the rest of the carrot stick into her mouth.

"What does the Celebrity Charity whatever have to do with Noel Jefferson?" Prue wadded up the paper napkins. Lemonade dripped through her fingers as she heaved the wad toward a litter container ten feet away. The soggy paper ball hit the rim of the wire-mesh container and started to fall toward the ground.

"Hey!" Phoebe's eyes flashed a warning when Prue raised her hand to telekinetically flip it inside the container. "If you and Piper don't stop with the power plays, the fact that we're witches is going to be breaking news."

"Sorry." Prue slid off the bench to pick up the soggy napkins.

Piper's gaze flicked skyward before she looked at Phoebe and shrugged. "When a power becomes second nature, you don't always stop to think before using it."

Phoebe understood that on an intellectual level but not in practice. Eventually, she'd have to remember that using her powers frivolously was against the rules, too. She couldn't control her ability to see the future or past, and she hadn't mastered the art of levitation to use it on reflex yet. Still, the day might come when she'd have to be careful not to take off for the wild blue yonder to rescue a cat stuck in a tree or something.

"Anybody want dessert?" Changing the subject, Phoebe stood and pulled a German chocolate cake from the picnic basket.

Prue leaned toward Piper when she sat down again. "Is Noel Jefferson going to be at the big event next Saturday?"

"Yep." Piper handed Phoebe a knife. "He and Stephen Tremaine are both giving speeches. Kind of a get-out-the-vote-and-while-you're-at-it-vote-for-me deal."

"Cool. Maybe I can get a couple of good shots of Jefferson for *415*. Just in case Gil needs them." Prue shrugged, but her casual attitude was as transparent as clean glass to Phoebe. Her elder sister wasn't batting a thousand in the game of love lately, either.

"Look out!" Piper shouted.

Phoebe dropped the knife as a black-and-white soccer ball fell out of the sky and bombed the cake. She jumped back, but not before her shirt was splattered by icing and sticky, shredded coconut. She cast a questioning glance at Piper and hissed, "Why didn't you freeze it?"

"Smashed cake does not qualify as a magical intervention emergency," Piper whispered back. Her gaze narrowed as a young girl about nine or ten years old ran up to the table.

The child's T-shirt and shorts were rumpled and damp with sweat. Her knees sported grass stains, and her face was smudged with dirt. She shuffled her feet and looked a little scared.

"Is this yours?" Smiling to put the girl at ease, Phoebe pulled the ball out of the crushed dessert. Chocolate icing and bits of chocolate cake stuck to the underside.

"Yeah. Sorry about your cake." The girl reached for the ball.

"That's okay—" When the child's hands touched the ball, Phoebe was rocked by a heart-stopping vision. Her muscles knotted, and she reeled as the images of imminent disaster played through her mind.

. . . *the little girl smashed to the ground, trampled by a shaggy beast, her scream cut short in a tangle of human and furry brown legs* . . .

"Thanks!" The girl turned and ran away.

Disoriented by the physical impact of the premonition, Phoebe lost precious seconds recovering. She struggled to regain her voice as Piper and Prue rushed to her side. "Wait!"

"What is it?" Prue asked as the child stopped and looked back.

"I'm not sure. Some kind of furry demon thing—" Phoebe glanced toward the pavilion where the birthday party was being held. A man in a cowboy hat was leading the pony toward a horse trailer parked in a nearby lot.

"What demon thing?" Piper pressed.

"The pony?" Phoebe hesitated uncertainly and shifted her gaze back to the girl, who tucked the ball under her arm and stared wistfully at the horse trailer.

"I wish I had a pony." The child's head suddenly rolled back. She swayed and sank to her grass-stained knees as her legs buckled.

Alarmed, Phoebe started toward her just as a loud squeal shattered the quiet afternoon. Her heart stopped when the pony balked at the trailer ramp, broke free of the handler, and galloped across the grass toward the stricken girl.

"Piper!" Phoebe screeched and broke into a run, determined to pull the girl out of harm's way. There were too many witnesses for Piper or Prue to use their powers safely.

And she wasn't going to make it in time.

It took only a second for Piper to realize what was happening and conclude that she couldn't freeze the pony without someone noticing. And there were too many people watching to freeze everything. The dozen adults and three dozen kids at the birthday party had all eyes glued on the runaway animal. The girl's teammates were unaware of the impending catastrophe until a hysterical man and woman started running to the rescue. Piper's power had grown stronger as time had passed, but it wasn't strong enough to handle this. Still, breaking news aside, she had to do something.

Prue's blue eyes widened as Piper's hands shot out.

"Move the kid!" Piper urged her older sister as the pony froze with one hoof on the ground.

Prue's eyes narrowed in concentration as she pulled the child toward Phoebe with a snap of her hand.

Piper unfroze the pony the instant the girl was clear.

The pony charged past Phoebe as she drew the stunned child into the protection of her arms. Phoebe glanced back and mouthed a thank-you.

Collapsing on the picnic table bench, Piper exhaled with relief and apprehension. The last thing

she needed was a headline the next morning pro-
claiming the "miraculous pony rescue." "Are we
toast?"

"Don't think so." Prue discreetly turned her telekinetic power on the pony, slowing his wild run
with a staying hand so the frantic cowboy could
catch him.

Phoebe released her hold on the girl when the
child's parents dropped down beside them. The girl
started to sob as her mother cradled and rocked her.
Her father, his face pale and drawn, mumbled
something Piper couldn't hear as Phoebe stood and
moved away.

A few of the other young soccer players were
watching the pony with wide, wondering eyes.
That didn't worry Piper too much. Kids were often
prone to exaggeration and telling tall tales, which
their parents weren't prone to believe. Near the
pavilion, however, a few huddled adults were
engaged in heated discussion and casting furtive
glances in her direction.

Resigned to weather whatever came next, Piper
surveyed the scene with a strange detachment. If
there was a price to be paid because someone had
noticed the real life stop-action pony, she'd figure
something out. The one price she wasn't willing to
pay was losing Leo because she had failed to act
when an innocent was in trouble.

She shivered with a sudden chill.

Enraged, he swept past the more-than-human
women and through the throng of people gathered

by the large hut, spreading a dread more intense than he had evoked when his spirit walked. He had been robbed of his demonic body in the distant past, but the vile female magic that had bound his essence had not stolen his power. Released into this strange land as a cohesive wisp of wind, he could still twist inconsequential human desire into cataclysmic harm.

And, as he had suspected when he'd fled the stone, the female shamans could still stop him.

He seethed because the child's frail form had not been battered, bloodied, and broken under the iron hooves of the rampaging beast.

He fumed because the lives the child touched would not be plunged into despair and destroyed by a horror they could never forget.

He whipped through the high branches of unfamiliar trees stripping them of leaves, maddened because the beast had failed and escaped uninjured.

He keened as he raced through the sky, infuriated because the witches had prevented the chaos set in motion by the child's desire. Their magic threatened the cascade of destruction triggered by the primary wish and his tenuous existence, but his resolve was greater than their power. He would have vengeance for all he had lost.

This time he would vanquish the witches.

CHAPTER
3

Phoebe settled into the sofa cushions and propped her fuzzy slippers on the coffee table. With her exams over and no classes until the following week, she was looking forward to a relaxing morning of doing nothing but catching up on the news and reading a racy gothic romance. She blew on a hot cup of coffee and hit the TV remote. Her aesthetic senses were immediately assaulted by a commercial that featured animated singing sausages.

"Too early for torture by low-budget marketing." Phoebe pushed the mute button, took a sip of coffee, and set the mug down. She picked up the paperback novel she had bought for a dollar at a used bookstore off campus. *Dark Passions at Midnight* was a poor substitute for muscled, manly arms, but it sure beat stuffing her head with the principles of thermodynamics.

Although she was interested in psychology and other studies about the human condition, which would help her understand the people in need of Charmed assistance, a working knowledge of the sciences might come in handy someday, too. Eventually, she'd have to decide on a paying career, and it couldn't hurt to be prepared for anything.

Right now she was content to share the heated but ill-fated love between Agatha Cross and Trevor Holcombe. According to the copy on the back of the book, Agatha was a poor but beautiful commoner who served as a nurse to Trevor's ailing father in Holcombe Manor. Agatha was also unaware that all the Holcombe women had succumbed to strange, premature deaths.

"Warm fuzzies *and* spine-chilling mystery. Perfect." As Phoebe flipped the book open to the prologue, the delicious aroma of freshly baked cinnamon rolls filled her nostrils. She looked up as Piper set a plate on the coffee table. "German chocolate cake yesterday and cinnamon rolls today. Are you deliberately trying to rot my teeth?"

Piper moved Phoebe's book to look at the cover. "No more than you're trying to rot your brain."

"My brain needs a break." Phoebe turned the paperback upside down on the arm of the sofa and lifted her cup. She looked longingly at the hot rolls and decided to pass. Working off the extra calories didn't fit into her plans to spend the day being lazy.

"How about we compromise with a little news."

Piper picked up the remote and turned the sound back on. Coffee cup in hand, she sat down beside Phoebe and tucked her long legs underneath her. "No classes today?"

"Nope. I've got five glorious days off." Phoebe raised her mug and grinned.

"Super." Piper gently hit Phoebe's mug with her own. "Then you can help me do the grocery shopping."

"Okay. Sure." Normally, Phoebe loved to shop— for anything. Today she would much rather stay home, pretending to be a woman of leisure, but she couldn't refuse to pitch in.

"Not terribly exciting, I know, but necessary," Piper said, noting Phoebe's disappointed frown. "Did I tell you Hard Crackers is going to play live at the Celebrity Charity Bazaar on Saturday?"

"Really? That's awesome!" Phoebe brightened. The local band was growing in popularity, in part because of the exposure they had gotten at Piper's club. Live music was bound to attract a crowd. "How much is that setting you back?"

"Not a dime." Piper beamed with satisfaction. "All they can eat and drink and a chance that one of the big time celebs will notice them."

"Cool." Shifting position, Phoebe frowned as Prue zipped down the hall and opened the front door. Phoebe stiffened at the sound of a siren, then realized it was a news clip on TV.

". . . two gang members and a man sitting in his living room were killed when the drive-by shooters opened fire," an announcer intoned. "The police are following leads supplied by eyewitnesses, but no arrests have been made."

Phoebe muted the sound again as the front door slammed closed. "Sorry, Piper, but I can't do murder and mayhem until after I finish my first cup of coffee."

"Ditto that." Piper sighed.

The reported incident wasn't anything to joke about, but sometimes humor was the only thing that kept Phoebe and her sisters sane. They faced more evil in a week than most people even knew existed.

"Did we make the front page?" Piper asked as Prue wandered in with the morning newspaper and perched on a chair.

Phoebe sat forward as Prue unfolded the paper, anxious to know if the runaway pony at the park yesterday had made news. She noted that Prue was still in her sleeping togs, too. Apparently, she didn't have any pressing engagements today, either. Phoebe's tension grew as her sister's blue eyes slowly scanned the front page. "Well?"

"Not a word." Smiling, Prue turned the paper so Phoebe and Piper could see.

Phoebe fell back against the cushions, but Piper wasn't as easily reassured.

"Flip!" Piper rigorously waved her hand at the paper. "Check *every* page."

"Yeah. Probably a good idea." Prue folded the front page back and creased it. "Would you mind getting me a cup of coffee?"

"I'll make an exception this morning," Piper teased. "I could use a warm-up anyway. Phoebe?"

"Sure, thanks." Phoebe handed Piper her cup, then turned a wary eye on Prue. She sat silently for a few minutes before impatience got the best of her. "Anything?"

"Just the usual so far, but I'm only on page four." Prue turned the paper over. "A mugging on Pacific Street, miscellaneous burglaries, some guy shot his girlfriend then killed himself and . . ."

"And?" Phoebe winced.

"A kid drowned in a community center pool." Prue cleared her throat. "But no mention of a pony suspended in midair."

"Good!" Gripping the handles of three full mugs in one hand, a serving trick Phoebe had yet to master, Piper handed one to each of her sisters and flopped back down on the sofa. "Last night I dreamed I was chased by a mob of angry parents and kids for freezing and unfreezing a merry-go-round over and over again."

Phoebe's smile faded as her gaze wandered to the muted TV. Coughing, soot-covered people in robes and pajamas were being rushed out of a burning apartment building. The camera panned across the street where dazed men and women clung to wide-eyed children and watched as their homes and possessions went up in flames.

"Only the truly good-hearted can have nightmares about carousels," Prue quipped.

"I guess the horror does lose something in the telling," Piper said, joking. "Just remind me not to go near the merry-go-round on Saturday."

"They're bringing in a merry-go-round?" Prue

turned over another page and snapped the paper to flatten it.

"The charity bazaar is being held at Boardwalk Beach right next to the Gold Coast Amusement Park." Piper paused, laughing softly. "Grams never liked taking us there, but I always loved it, especially the carousel."

"One of her, three of us." Prue smiled, remembering. "We were a little hard to keep track of, even for an accomplished witch."

Still focused on the TV screen, Phoebe listened to the banter with half an ear. The news team had segued from the apartment fire to a flood in the Midwest. Instead of almost being incinerated, people cast adrift on makeshift rafts and small boats paddled past houses filled with water. When the picture of a small boy, who had been missing in a national park for three days, flashed on the screen, she picked up the remote and turned the set off.

"Oh, no!" Prue scowled at the paper.

"What?" Phoebe and Piper asked simultaneously. Phoebe's coffee sloshed when she jerked to attention, spilling several drops on her long T-shirt.

"My favorite boutique is having a sale, and my card is maxed," Prue said. "I could really use a pair of new boots."

"Don't scare me like that." Phoebe sagged. "I've had about all the bad news I can take for one morning."

"What bad news?" Prue looked bewildered as she folded the paper and dropped it on the floor.

"All of it!" Gripping her cup, Phoebe shook her head.

"I obviously missed something," Piper said.

"Fires and floods, muggings and lost kids." Phoebe shuddered. She had awakened in a great mood, but the news reports in the paper and on TV had demolished it. Natural disaster and human malevolence waged a relentless war against the helpless. At least the Charmed Ones could fight the demonic evil they encountered.

Phoebe caught her lip in her teeth to keep it from trembling. Sometimes the depressing reality was more than she could stand, made worse because she so often experienced someone else's pain and terror in her own mind. She was glad she could help the people her power touched, but the ability to see the future was as much a curse as it was a blessing.

"Are you okay?" Concerned, Piper rested a hand on Phoebe's knee.

"Yeah, it's just that—" Phoebe sighed, thinking about the little girl they had saved from the stampeding pony because her power had given them a warning. Without that lead time, the girl would have been maimed or worse under the pony's shod hooves. "I wish my visions weren't so selective because then we could keep more of this awful stuff from happening."

Phoebe's stomach suddenly heaved with nausea, and a rush of dizziness made her head spin. Her coffee mug slipped from her hand as she gasped and doubled over.

"Phoebe!" Piper threw her arms around her stricken sister and let the mug land, unfrozen, on the carpet.

"What is it?" Prue jumped from her chair and knelt down by the sofa. "A vision?"

"Sick," Phoebe muttered. That was an understatement, she thought. The wretched feeling had hit her so fast and with such force that she felt as if someone had blindsided her with a triple whammy spell.

"Maybe we'd better call the doctor." Prue dashed to the phone.

"Wait." Phoebe held up a hand to stop Prue from dialing when the sickening sensations began to fade. She took a couple of deep breaths and sat up slowly. "It's going away."

"I need specifics, Phoebe," Piper said, probably a little more sharply than she intended. She did that when she was really worried. "What's going away?"

"Super queasy stomach, dizzy." Phoebe wiped a fine sheen of sweat from her brow and took another deep breath as her head cleared. "Weird."

"Too weird." Prue sat on the coffee table and picked the mug up from the floor. "One minute you're fine and the next you're in agony? I don't like it."

"Agony is a little extreme." Phoebe looked at the damp coffee stain on the carpet. "And maybe it's not that weird, now that I think about it."

"I'm listening." Piper folded her arms and fixed Phoebe with a skeptical gaze.

"I've been really pushing it lately, studying for my exams and not getting enough sleep, and everything," Phoebe explained. "The strain must have finally caught up with me."

"You're always pushing it, Phoebe," Prue pointed out. "Between your school assignments, hanging out at the club—"

"Which she doesn't have to do," Piper interjected.

"I like going to P3," Phoebe countered. "A girl's gotta have some fun."

"Yes, but most girls aren't vanquishing demons on a regular basis, either." Prue eyed Phoebe with unguarded concern. "You hardly ever get enough sleep."

"Okay," Phoebe admitted, "but I haven't eaten since our picnic yesterday, either. It's obviously an open-and-shut case of too much coffee on an empty stomach." To make her point, she grabbed a cinnamon roll and took a bite.

Prue frowned at Piper. "Do you buy that?"

"I don't know." Piper raised an eyebrow as Phoebe devoured the roll. "I'd like to believe it. Sick is much easier to deal with than the alternatives, if you get my drift."

"I don't think it was magic. I've been nauseous and dizzy from hunger before." When Prue and Piper frowned, Phoebe quickly clarified. "I wasn't exactly rolling in money in New York, remember?"

Piper went rigid. "I didn't know you were starving!"

"Not starving," Phoebe said. She didn't want to

open old wounds, especially since her sisters had bailed her out financially more than once before she had returned to San Francisco. "Just hungry enough to get light-headed with an upset stomach every once in a while."

"Are you sure?" Prue asked.

"Positive." Phoebe nodded and chewed as her stomach settled. She was still a little shaky, but she was certain the sudden attack was nothing more than her body reacting to the physical and emotional stress of cramming for exams the past two weeks. Compounded by some really nasty demon fighting, she added mentally. "I'm fine. Really."

Athulak, as he had been known long ago, resented the loss of his physical being. He had stalked the dank forests near the great river for centuries, a demon in human form, immune to the weapons wielded by his savage subjects, sustained by the fear and terror he created from their passions. He would not have adapted so easily as a man walking among them now. Human weaknesses had not changed, but the world people lived in had been altered beyond recognition.

Humans, who had once struggled to sustain their fragile existence against the more powerful elements, had taken control. They no longer depended on the hunt or the river or cultivating patches of land for food. They did not cower in mud huts, fearful of storms, nor were they confined by the limits of human speed and endurance. They lived in sturdy structures large and small, and com-

manded mighty machines that labored and carried
them over vast distances, faster than the wind he
had become.

But for all their miraculous achievements, they
were still human, and his power to disrupt and affect
human destiny had not been diminished.

The witch, however, was human and more,
Athulak realized as he hung near the ceiling of the
room she occupied with the others. If he still inhabited the body of a man, the strange objects the three
female shamans possessed might have captured his
interest, but the box full of shadow forms and the
artifacts were of no use to him. The absence of
material distraction was an advantage he was just
beginning to appreciate as he watched and waited.

"Maybe you should rest, Phoebe." The woman
who could stop time gathered the drinking bowls
and stood up. "I can handle the grocery shopping."

"Maybe, but I'm not in the mood for lying
around the house anymore." The seer turned to the
third woman. "How about you, Prue? Feel like
going out?"

"I'm not sure the supermarket qualifies as 'going
out,' " Piper said.

The blue-eyed woman picked up a heavy pack
lying by the entrance. "Actually, I'd love to, but I've
still got to develop the Tremaine film. Gil wants the
proofs tomorrow."

"That's too bad." The seer smiled.

"Isn't it?" Piper glanced at Prue as she picked up
the platter of bread. "Will the pictures of P3 be
ready for Saturday?"

"Absolutely." Slinging the pack over her shoulder, the woman who moved things with her mind headed toward the door. "And if you don't like them, we can always take more tonight or tomorrow."

"I hate it when you cut things so close," Piper said as she followed Prue out.

Athulak drifted closer when the seer known as Phoebe threw her head back and closed her eyes. He shimmered, anxious for a sign that the cascade had begun, but there was none.

Impatient and annoyed, he whipped past her and through the slits of a metal covering on the wall. As he sped through the dusty metal tunnel that led to another vent and the outside, he reminded himself that she was a witch. She would be consumed and destroyed, but it would take time.

CHAPTER
4

Piper set her bag in the child's seat of the grocery cart as she and Phoebe walked through the automatic doors into the store. She pulled out her shopping list and gave it a quick once-over to refresh her memory.

"What's with all the goodies?" Phoebe glanced at the list, then stepped back to follow as Piper turned right and headed toward the bakery. "Are we having a party?"

"No, we're not having a party," Piper said. "I'm either going to be lonely for Leo with all my favorite things in the world to eat or I'm going to stuff Leo with all my favorite things in the world to eat when he shows up."

"Cool! Either way, I win." Phoebe grinned. "I love all that stuff, too."

"Guess we'd better double everything, then." Piper caught an edge of irritation creeping into her voice and realized she was being unfair. Phoebe wasn't trying to belittle her longing for Leo. She really did love all of Grams's recipes.

"Triple," Phoebe said. "We can't binge on ham rolls and black bread with cream cheese without Prue."

"Wouldn't think of it." Piper softened her tone and steered the conversation into less sensitive territory. "Would you remind me to call my wholesaler later? I special ordered some fancy finger foods for the bazaar and I want to make sure there're no mix-ups."

"What kind of finger foods?" Phoebe asked.

"Canapés, cheeses, summer sausages, breads with some seasoned specialty spreads—"

"Whoa!" Phoebe held up a hand. "Wouldn't chips and dips be easier? And cheaper?"

"Easier, cheaper, and totally tacky," Piper said, annoyed.

"Yes, but P3 is a *club*," Phoebe pressed. "Cool crowd, great bands, dancing. Nobody goes there to eat."

"Most of the people at the charity bazaar won't *know* P3 is a great dance club unless we can *get* them to our booth." Piper rolled her eyes and handed Phoebe the list over her shoulder without looking back. "So we've got to have cool food."

"Okay, you're the boss." Phoebe didn't sound convinced as she took the paper and followed Piper toward the bakery counter straight ahead.

"Let's get some of those blueberry mini-muffins—" Piper stopped in her tracks when Phoebe grabbed the back of her blouse.

"Hold it!" Phoebe's fingers tightened when Piper tried to pull away.

"What are you—" Piper's question was cut short when a speeding grocery cart cut in front of her from a side aisle. The reckless shopper, an unkempt man wearing torn jeans and a dirty T-shirt, didn't look her way. He grabbed a bag of rolls without slowing down and just kept going.

Incensed, Piper checked an impulse to freeze the guy before he plowed into something or someone and did some serious damage. Another realization kicked in that seemed more important.

If Phoebe hadn't stopped her, the supermarket maniac would have rammed his cart right into her.

Piper looked back at her sister. "You knew?"

"Yeah. I got a flash when you gave me this." Phoebe held up Piper's grocery list. "Major impact with that bozo's cart. Wham! Right into the coffee cakes on that counter. Instant broken wrist."

"He hit me that hard?" Piper shivered. The grocery store was one of the few places that had always seemed like a haven from the violence that plagued their lives. She had given up longing for the days when she had been just an ordinary young woman who wanted to fall in love, get married, and have a couple of kids. She tried to live as though nothing had changed as much as being a witch with a mission and a supernatural husband allowed. Still, she resented the intrusion of danger into her safe space.

"*Almost* hit you that hard," Phoebe corrected.

"Right. Thanks." Piper decided not to let the incident ruin her day. The man was a jerk, but he wasn't some despicable evil that required the Charmed Ones' undivided attention. Between missing Leo and making preparations for the P3 booth at the Celebrity Charity Bazaar, she really wasn't in the mood to drop everything to battle a demon.

"Are you okay?" Phoebe asked, frowning. "You look mad. Not that I'd blame you."

"No, I'm fine. Just a little anxious because there's so much to do before Saturday." Piper smiled. "Let's get this done and get out of here."

"I won't argue with that." Phoebe checked both ways to make sure the cross aisle was clear, then motioned Piper to move on.

As they wove their way up and down the aisles, Piper's mind kept wandering back to the near collision that hadn't happened because Phoebe had had a vision. This wasn't the first time Phoebe's power of premonition had saved her or Prue and it wouldn't be the last, but Piper was reminded of just how abnormal their lives really were. When it got right down to it, no matter how much she wanted to be "normal," it wasn't possible. She couldn't even plan a cozy dinner for two with Leo because she never knew when he was going to orb in—or orb out again.

"Want to pick up some of these for Leo?" Phoebe dropped two boxes of oatmeal raisin granola bars into the cart.

"Have you expanded into mind reading?" Piper asked, amused. "I was just thinking about Leo."

"You're always thinking about Leo," Phoebe teased. She dropped a third box of granola bars into the cart. "I hate it when I get a granola craving and we don't have any."

Piper winced. Leo had a habit of helping himself to anything in the Halliwell pantry, which seemed only fair since he was their guardian White Lighter and Piper's husband. However, she made a mental note to stock up on his favorite snacks in the future. She and her sisters had enough problems without bickering over the availability of granola bars.

"You really miss him, don't you?" Phoebe asked.

The question caught Piper off guard. She and her sisters were close, but she didn't always tell them what was bothering her until circumstances forced it out of her. Phoebe and Prue had accepted their powers and the enormous responsibility that went with them a lot more readily than she had. She felt a little guilty because she had had more trouble reconciling her personal life with their higher calling. She wasn't proud of it, but she couldn't ignore it, either. Even so, the cereal aisle of the grocery store wasn't the right place for a serious discussion of her personal failings.

"Yes, but I also know he'll be back as soon as he can." Piper pointed down the aisle. "I think the canned black bread is down there."

"Let's stock up," Phoebe said. "My mouth is already watering."

"Not a problem." Piper, like Phoebe and Prue, loved the moist black bread and cream cheese snack sandwiches Grams had made for them when they were kids. Piper had always appreciated her grandmother's domestic, no-magic streak, but the simple recipes satisfied something much deeper than a culinary craving. They helped bridge the gap between this world and the next, now that Grams had passed on.

Phoebe patted her flat stomach. "I'm going to have to spend all next week working out."

"You could skip the snacks," Piper suggested.

"Don't think so," Phoebe said without hesitation. "Life is way too short not to indulge once in a while."

Piper couldn't argue with that. Her mind wandered right back to Leo as she followed Phoebe up and down the aisles. She did miss him—a lot—and sometimes she wondered if he realized how hard the separations were on her. Until she had orbed out to the White Lighter headquarters "up there," she hadn't known that time passed much more slowly there than it did in the mortal world. She hadn't seen Leo in two weeks, but less than a day had passed for him. Unless he's on another assignment here, she reminded herself.

"All we need are some fresh vegetables and we're done." Phoebe put pen to paper and scratched two pounds of thinly sliced deli ham off the list.

"Great!" Piper abandoned her momentary lapse into self-pity. The separations were hard, but she was grateful the powers-that-be had given her and Leo a chance to work things out. She smiled at Phoebe. "Then we can go home and do the fun part."

"The eating part." Phoebe held up a fresh bundle

of broccoli for Piper's approval. "With a little ranch dressing?"

"Perfect." Piper gave a thumbs-up on the broccoli, then pointed to a stock boy who was restocking behind Phoebe. "Grab a couple of those scallion bunches, will you?"

"You got it." Phoebe handed the broccoli to Piper and sidled up to the teenager. "Can I have two of those before you stuff them behind the old ones?"

"Sure." Obviously flustered by Phoebe's good nature and good looks, the boy fumbled with a plastic bag, counted out two bunches of scallions, and shoved the bag toward Phoebe. "Here you go."

Piper looked away. The boy was embarrassed enough without adding to his discomfort by gawking. After a few seconds, when Phoebe didn't bounce up with the scallions, she looked back as the boy pushed through the stockroom doors with the produce cart.

The bag of scallions was on the floor.

Phoebe was clinging to the edge of the counter, her knuckles white with strain. Her eyes were closed, and her breath came in short, ragged gasps.

Alarmed by the effects of another vision, Piper sprang toward her sister.

"What is it, Phoebe?"

Phoebe barely heard Piper through the images that had flooded her mind when she brushed the stock boy's hand. The vision had hit her like a physical blow and held her mind in a viselike grip that was augmented by the panic inherent in a sense of helplessness.

No scream escaped the ambushed boy as bone and muscle were pulverized between massive, moving walls.

Beads of sweat dampened Phoebe's face as the image blinked out. The onslaught of a second vision following so close to the first left her more shaken than usual. Head throbbing, she tightened her aching fingers on the counter, which kept her upright as her knees began to buckle.

Piper grabbed Phoebe's arms to steady her. "What's happening?"

As the effects dissipated, Phoebe struggled to collect herself and looked around. "Where'd he go?"

"The stock boy?" Piper asked. "Back there."

"Come on. He's going to get squashed if we don't stop it." Phoebe staggered for the doors. She didn't have time to go into detail. If they were too late to avert the whole calamity, Piper's ability to freeze was the teenager's only hope.

"Stop what?" Piper was on Phoebe's heels as she burst into the large warehouse area of the store.

"That." Phoebe stared at the huge black semi backing up to the loading dock. The docking bay was about thirty feet wide, and the driver had positioned the truck in the middle. The day before, disaster had ridden on the back of one runaway pony. Today it was packed into hundreds of tons of horsepower under the hood of a sleek rig called Thunder & Stone.

Phoebe shifted her attention to the stock boy, who was standing on the edge of the raised loading platform with a man in rolled-up shirtsleeves and a tie. A manager, she surmised as her eye darted to another man sitting in an idling forklift nearby. She hesitated, realizing something about the scene wasn't right. In her vision, the boy had been on the ground in the bay and the truck had pinned him to the dock.

As though on cue, the manager glanced down over the edge of the loading platform. "Get that crate out of there, Barry."

"Okay." As Barry jumped into the bay, the manager turned toward the forklift.

"No!" Phoebe shouted. "Get him out of there!"

Barry looked up, totally forgetting about the truck that was still backing toward the dock.

"Sorry, ladies!" the manager called out. "You can't be back here. Authorized—"

"Piper!" Phoebe turned frantic eyes on her sister. Freezing a tractor-trailer truck and four people was a little more than Piper was usually called on to handle. Okay, a lot more, Phoebe thought, but they had no choice. If they didn't act, Barry would be crushed. "Now, please!"

"Right." Piper grimaced as she threw up her hands.

Phoebe was already running toward Barry when the whole scene came to a stop.

"We've got to hurry," Piper said as they reached the edge of the dock. "This was a pretty big stop order, and I don't know how long it will hold."

"Let's just hope it's long enough." Phoebe knelt down and lowered herself to the drive, wishing

Prue had come along. Barry probably would have suffered some painful bumps and bruises after Prue yanked him clear with a power pull, but that was better than being flattened by a truck. And now, Phoebe thought as she clamped onto the boy's arm, she was in the crash zone, too.

Piper jumped down and grabbed Barry's other arm. "Come on, big boy."

Piper and Phoebe pulled just as the truck's engine roared to life.

"What? Where?" The manager sputtered when Piper and Phoebe seemed to disappear before his eyes. Most of the time they tried to get back into position before anyone unfroze, but it wasn't always possible.

Not our biggest problem, Phoebe realized as Barry stumbled backward. She and Piper went down with him as he fell.

The truck brakes squealed as the driver brought the rig to a halt against the dock.

Buried under the stunned stock boy, Phoebe whispered to Piper. "Encore."

Piper nodded, raised her hands and froze everyone again. She got to her feet and blew a stray strand of hair off her forehead. "Now what?"

Grunting, Phoebe struggled out from under Barry and stood up. She had an idea with about a million-in-one chance of working, but she couldn't think of anything else. "Run."

Piper didn't argue as Phoebe urged her up the ladder at the end of the bay. They hit the platform running, barreling past the immobile workers and

through the doors back into the produce department. They slowed to a fast walk as the doors
swung closed behind them and hurried back to
their grocery cart.

"The sooner we get out of here the better," Piper
said as she grabbed the cart.

"What about the veggies?" Phoebe glanced back
as Piper headed up the dish and laundry detergent
aisle.

"We'll swing by Sam's vegetable store on the way
home," Piper called back over her shoulder.

When the doors into the warehouse started to
swing open, Phoebe ducked into the aisle out of
sight. With any kind of luck, Barry, the manager,
and the forklift driver would assume their strange
vanishing act had never actually happened. That
particular quirk of human nature often worked to
the Halliwells' benefit when they couldn't totally
cover their magical tracks. However, she didn't
want to tempt fate by sticking around to find out if
it was going to work this time. Phoebe dashed
after Piper, who was already halfway down the
aisle.

To hurry things along at the checkout counter,
Phoebe unloaded the cart while Piper helped an
elderly man bag. By the time she put the last few
cans of black bread on the conveyor, she relaxed.
The warehouse manager's attention had probably
been diverted by Barry's close call with the back of
the truck. On-the-job accidents, workers' comp, and
insurance rates were a higher priority than mysterious, disappearing customers.

"Good. You're done. We need that." Piper pulled the cart forward to be loaded with bagged groceries.

"Except for this!" Phoebe handed the last can of black bread to the cashier. As their fingertips touched, she was seized with another premonition. She swayed slightly as her head swam with an image that flashed by so fast she wasn't quite sure what she had seen.

... *blood seeping from a wound* ...

"You okay, miss?" the cashier asked.

Piper's head snapped around. Her eyes narrowed.

"Fine." Phoebe recovered quickly from the temporary disorientation. All her visions were disturbing, but there was no sense of real urgency associated with the mini version she had just experienced. She smiled at the matronly cashier as Piper paid the bill. "Don't touch anything sharp, okay?"

"Okay." The woman looked at her askance and handed Piper her change.

Piper frowned. "Ready?"

"More than." Rolling her eyes, Phoebe waved Piper to move out. She looked back as the automatic doors opened.

The cashier started to straighten a stack of sale flyers on the counter. She yelped and shook her finger as blood seeped out of a paper cut.

Prue loved the tranquility of the darkroom. With the exception of the occasional evil intruder or life-or-death interruption, her professional domain was isolated from whatever was going on outside. Even her sisters, who had no compunction about barging into the bathroom or into her bedroom to borrow her clothes, followed the darkroom do-not-enter rule. It wasn't just a question of spoiled photos and lost time if light got in at an inopportune moment. They respected her space—unless there was a crisis.

She was incredibly lucky, Prue thought as her gaze flicked to the proofs of Stephen Tremaine hanging above the solution pans. After years of working for someone else, she had taken the risky plunge to freelance. Photography had always been a passion, and the career move was exhilarating, challenging, and very scary.

"As though I didn't have enough scary in my life," Prue muttered as she began processing the last few shots she had snapped of the congressional candidate. The uncertainty and fear she faced every day because she was a witch probably wouldn't change, but the uncertainty and fear presented by her new profession lessened with every assignment she completed to the magazine's satisfaction. The transition from steady paycheck to being paid by the job, when there was a job, hadn't been easy. Getting into the good graces of the editor at 415 had helped, though, and the Tremaine assignment was crucial to staying in the game.

Gil and Tremaine will both love these shots, Prue thought as she hung up another picture to dry. The lighting and angles softened Tremaine's austere bone structure and smoothed the rough texture of his aging skin, which should appeal to his vanity. In the photo she had just processed, she had managed to capture him in a moment of admiration for the primitive stone figure. The expression produced a desirable quality of human awe he didn't display in person. If she didn't know anything about the man or his corporate-driven agenda, the photo might have convinced her to vote for him.

"Unfortunately, Mr. Stephen Tremaine, you're a no-go on every level." Prue sighed as she addressed the man's picture. "No vote, no chemistry, too bad."

Prue frowned as she stared at the photo. The light gray speck on the crude eye carved into the stone was so minuscule that she hadn't noticed it at first glance. Now that it was apparent, the tiny flaw leaped off the paper. Concerned, she quickly finished processing the remaining three photos. Her impish mood evaporated as the speck enlarged with each successive shot. In the last one, the flaw looked like a faint plume of smoke.

A defect in the film? Prue wondered as she studied the shots that finished up the roll. She had never had a problem with the professional grade film before, but that didn't mean a problem wasn't possible.

Just as something more sinister wasn't *impossible*, she thought on closer inspection.

Tremaine had been talking about his campaign against Noel Jefferson when she had finished the session, and the pictures had caught several emotions during the course of the short conversation. He had segued from pride in the rare stone statue to a variety of expressions regarding his campaign: concern, determination, anger, and pensive thought.

No, not pensive, Prue realized remembering back. Tremaine had zoned out for a second on her last shot. He had dismissed the fleeting event as nothing, but in the past she had been blindsided by too many nothings that had turned into dangerous somethings to ignore it.

Troubled, Prue examined each photo again, but this time she concentrated on the flaw. The expanding gray shadow was positioned in the same section of each photo, which did not eliminate faulty film as the cause. On the other hand, that didn't *prove* the film was responsible.

Planting her hands on her hips, Prue exhaled with frustration. A problem with the film was the most logical explanation and the easiest to accept, but she wasn't quite ready to buy it. Maybe her lens had failed. And of course, the specter of a supernatural source always hovered as a possibility.

"Supernatural based on what?" Prue asked herself aloud. She felt a little foolish for imagining the worst, but she'd rather know one way or the other. She was more suspicious than her sisters, a trait that had proven to be valuable too often. "And this leopard can't change its spots now."

Intrigued, Prue pulled a magnifying glass out of a drawer and used it to study the defect in each shot. She didn't identify the one similarity all the photos shared until she was halfway through a second, more intense scrutiny of the series. Tremaine's head and upper body, his arm, hand, and the primitive statue were positioned about the same in all four pictures with only slight variations. His head was tilted back more in one, and his arm was lower in another. The smoky flaw, however, began and elongated from the same point in the statue's rounded eye.

Puzzled, Prue put the magnifying glass away and removed her apron. She didn't believe in freak coincidence, but she had absolutely no reason to believe it wasn't the cause of the problems with the photos. Still, for safety's sake, it couldn't hurt to try to figure it out.

Anxious to get busy, Prue stopped in the kitchen to put a kettle on for tea, then headed for the living room to get her camera bag. She had purchased several rolls of film at the same time and quickly loaded her camera. The test wouldn't be conclusive if the flaw didn't show up in the new shots, but she could definitely find out if the lens was to blame.

With her tea made and camera in hand, Prue pulled the shades on the front windows in the living room to re-create the lighting in Tremaine's library the day before. Then she began snapping shots of the Halliwell furniture.

CHAPTER
5

Piper parked in front of the small produce market, turned off the engine, and clamped down on Phoebe's arm as she moved to open the door. "Not so fast."

"What?" Phoebe blinked, bewildered. "Is something wrong?"

"You tell me." Crossing her arms, Piper fixed Phoebe with a piercing stare. Her effervescent younger sister, who usually drove her to distraction with nonstop babbling, had said hardly a word since they'd left the supermarket.

"Tell you what?" Phoebe frowned. "And turn off the Grams stare. It makes me feel like I'm five years old again."

"Sorry." Piper moved one hand up to cup her chin and tried to soften her stern expression. She had never liked their grandmother's all-knowing stare, either. As a child, she had been certain Grams was tuned in to some mysterious force that spied and reported on their every move. It wasn't until she had grown up that she realized their own guilty behavior had usually given them away.

"Like that time Grams told me not to wear my new patent leather shoes outside to play." A wistful smile dawned on Phoebe's face. "I cleaned the mud off the shiny black part with a towel and didn't figure out until years later that the towel and the mud on the soles had tipped her off."

"I remember," Piper said.

"I thought she really *did* have eyes in the back of her head." Phoebe laughed.

"And changing the subject won't help you with *me* any more than it helped with Grams back then." Piper leveled Phoebe with another pointed stare.

"What does *that* mean?" Phoebe looked genuinely confused.

"Until your trip down memory lane, you've been awfully quiet," Piper said. "One thing that hasn't changed in the past twenty years is that you only stop talking when you've got something heavy on your mind."

"That obvious, huh?" Phoebe glanced out the side window, sighed, then looked at Piper and shrugged. "It's probably nothing."

"Phoebe!" Piper raised her voice in exasperation. "We're not budging until you talk, even if the sour cream curdles before we get home."

"Threats will get you nowhere," Phoebe

quipped. Her grin faded when Piper didn't laugh. "Okay, it's the visions. Too many, too close together, and too totally weird."

Piper stiffened. Anything unusual regarding their powers was cause for concern. "How many and how weird?"

"Three at the supermarket," Phoebe explained, "ranging from a paper cut to a crushed stock boy."

"*Almost* crushed stock boy and a close call with getting caught stopping time. Not to mention an almost broken wrist for me." Not fun, Piper thought, but she didn't understand why that was bothering her sister. Normally, Phoebe took living dangerously in stride. "I don't understand the weird part."

"I *saw* the cashier cut her finger." A touch of anxiety crept into Phoebe's voice.

"And that's bad?" Piper was still lost.

"I don't know. It's just that it was such a *little* thing." A worried scowl darkened Phoebe's face. "My visions are *never* trivial."

"Well, apparently, they are now." Piper frowned, too, but she was puzzled. She didn't want to belittle Phoebe's concern, but she didn't see the problem. Her own ability to freeze and Prue's telekinetic strength had increased dramatically since their powers had been restored. They would have been a lot stronger if Grams hadn't cast a spell to make the sisters' powers dormant for their protection as kids. Prue could even astral project at will. Phoebe had acquired the power to levitate herself, but that was a gift from a vanquished bad guy and not a natural—

"Yeah," Phoebe agreed, "but why?

Piper slapped her forehead. "Maybe because *your* power is getting more fine tuned, stronger, like Prue's telekinetic whammy."

Phoebe brightened immediately. "You think?"

"Have you got a better theory?" Piper dropped the car keys into her purse.

"Nope. Let's shop. I've suddenly got a craving for fresh fruit." Obviously relieved, Phoebe jumped out of the car and followed Piper into the store. "So what's the scoop on the new bartender?"

"Rick. Grad student, psychology, working on a thesis that has something to do with pop culture, which is why he wanted the job." Piper waved at Sam, the store's owner, and slipped the handles of a plastic basket over her arm.

"Oh." Phoebe frowned. "So maybe his interest in me wasn't romantic. Maybe he just thought I might make a good research subject."

"Maybe. Don't know," Piper teased. "I guess you'll just have to meet him to find out."

"Lab rat or dinner date?" Phoebe grimaced. "I'll have to think about it."

While Phoebe wandered off to inspect the fruit section, Piper browsed through the bins of fresh vegetables. Sam's produce market had grown from a small storefront into a sprawling establishment. As she made her selections, Piper was glad that circumstances had forced her to make the extra stop. Sam's produce was fresher and less expensive than the supermarket's. P3 was starting to boom, but with Prue freelancing and Phoebe going to school, every dollar saved was a bonus.

"Hurry up, Phoebe!" Piper called when she had finished. She pointed toward the front of the store, where Sam was making change from an old-fashioned cash register.

"One more minute!" Phoebe picked up a quart of strawberries and hurried toward her.

Shaking her head, Piper stood to wait her turn behind a young woman with a toddler in a stroller. The little boy had bright red hair that clashed with the red-checkered shirt he wore under blue denim bib overalls. Green lollipop goo ran down the stick to his fingers when he held out the treat.

"Pop!" The boy giggled.

"That's okay. You eat it." Piper smiled when the boy's mother looked back. "Cute kid."

"Thanks." The woman set her bag on top of the stroller canopy. "Come on, Nathan. Daddy's taking us to lunch and we're late."

Piper set her basket on the wooden counter, wondering if the woman always fed her son candy before meals.

"How you doin', Piper?" Sam's gold tooth gleamed in the sun when he grinned. Sixty, with the stubble of a white beard, he wore baggy pants held up by suspenders and a plaid shirt with a torn pocket.

"I'm fine, Sam. And you?" Piper wasn't sure how long Sam had been selling fruits and vegetables. His store had been there as far back as she could remember, and he would be missed if he ever retired.

Cradling a bag of oranges and a bunch of barely

ripe bananas in one arm, Phoebe stopped at the end
of the counter. She balanced the container of strawberries on top of the bananas and held it steady
with her chin so she could grab a couple of kiwi.

Behind Phoebe, the young mother finished
arranging her bundles and started to push the
stroller toward the door.

"Uh-oh!" Phoebe yelped.

Before Piper could react, the young woman
turned and caught the basket of red berries before it
fell.

"Thanks," Phoebe said with a sheepish grin. "I
can be a real klutz."

"Happens to me all the time." After setting the
strawberries on the counter, the woman put her
hand in her pocket as she pushed the stroller out
the door. When she pulled out her keys, a pacifier
flipped out of her pocket.

Awkwardly Phoebe managed to unload the
oranges and bananas on the counter, then scooped
up the pacifier. She was instantly caught in the grip
of another vision. Unbalanced by bending over, she
fell to her hands and knees with her eyes closed.

"Phoebe?" Sam's eyes widened.

Piper ran to her sister and knelt down, her own
heart pounding as she saw the pacifier. She was
anxious to know what was flashing through
Phoebe's mind, but she had to wait until she
snapped out of the daze. One thing was clear without Phoebe's confirmation.

Some kind of disaster was going to befall
Nathan.

"Come on, Phoebe," Piper urged. Her pulse rate had doubled by the time her sister came to. "What?"

"Car accident." Alert and now on her feet, Phoebe glanced toward the street. Nathan's mother had just pulled her steel gray minivan into traffic. "Let's go."

"Hold my stuff, Sam!" Piper called over her shoulder as she ran after Phoebe. She had the car door closed, her seat belt fastened, and the engine running before Phoebe buckled up. "Where?"

"I'm not sure." Phoebe craned her neck to track the minivan down the busy boulevard. "Hurry, before we lose them!"

Piper's stomach knotted, remembering Nathan's cheerful face. She wouldn't be able to sleep if anything happened to him because she and Phoebe didn't arrive in time. Gravel flew as she backed up, and the tires spun when she shifted into drive. She slammed on the brakes at the exit and pounded her fist on the steering wheel. A steady stream of traffic whizzed by in both directions.

"Come on, Piper!" Phoebe's voice was tight with urgency, her gaze still trained on the van stopped at a traffic light. "That light could change any second and we might lose them."

"Hang on!" Piper gunned the engine and shot into the street with little margin for error as a pickup truck roared toward her. She slowed to let a yellow convertible speeding in the opposite direction pass, then gunned the engine again.

"Watch it!" Phoebe cringed, but she didn't take her eyes off the gray minivan.

The driver of the pickup truck slammed on the brakes and just missed clipping Piper's bumper as she yanked the steering wheel hard to the left. The car fishtailed as Piper whipped into the flow of traffic. As soon as it straightened out, she zipped into the right-hand lane.

"Where'd you learn how to do that?" Phoebe asked with a hint of admiration. "Crash course in stunt driving?"

"*Smokey and the Bandit.*" Piper wiped one of her sweaty hands on her pants, then switched her grip on the steering wheel and wiped the other. The classic car-chase movie was a secret favorite. "I saw it five times."

"Uh-huh." Phoebe raised herself up from the seat and pointed out the windshield. "They're turning right."

"Got it." Piper rode the tail of the car in front of her and turned right just as the light turned red. Three cars separated them from the minivan cruising in the right lane ahead.

With the van in sight and the daredevil phase of the mission behind her, Piper watched for an opening to pass and shifted her focus to the imminent accident. "What should we be looking for?"

"I'm not sure. The van just kind of got mangled in a blur of red." Phoebe caught her lip in her teeth and scanned the surrounding area when the minivan stopped at another red light. "I don't have a clue, Piper. Nothing looks familiar."

"So maybe it doesn't happen right away," Piper suggested as she brought the car to a stop. Either that or Phoebe's brain had gone mushy from over-load. Four visions in a couple of hours had to be a record.

Phoebe frowned, shook her head. "No, I'm pretty sure—"

The blare of an approaching siren cut her off.

"That's it!" Phoebe's eyes bulged with sudden horror. "Fire truck. Coming from over there." She pointed toward the cross street on the left. Dozens of cars pulled over or halted in the middle of the road even though they had the green light. "She's going to pull out in front of it."

Piper fought off panic as the hopelessness of the situation hit her. With three cars between them and the minivan and less than a minute to go before impact, stopping the collision was impossible—except for her power. There was no way she could freeze the entire intersection and everything in it, Piper realized. Her power just wasn't that strong.

But she couldn't just sit and do nothing.

"Your turn to drive, Phoebe." Without taking time to explain, Piper threw open the door and jumped out. The blast of the siren grew louder as she ran between two rows of cars toward the van.

From the corner of her eye, Piper saw the large fire truck race down the center turn lane past the stopped traffic. Siren screeching, the red giant entered the intersection—just as the gray minivan rolled forward to make a right turn.

Piper was stunned. Was Nathan's mom in such a hurry to meet her husband she was willing to risk her life and her son's? Or, perhaps, she couldn't hear the siren because her car stereo was cranked or Nathan was crying. All the possible explanations rose in Piper's mind as she raised her hands and froze the van.

The fire truck roared past as the traffic light changed.

Emotionally and physically drained, Piper unfroze the van, which lurched to a halt as the woman reacted to the startling gap in her perceptions. She probably had no idea how close she and Nathan had come to sudden death.

Emotionally and physically drained, Piper's heart lurched when the cars behind the van leaned on their horns. She hurried back to the car, slid into the passenger seat, and sagged.

"Nice going." Phoebe grinned and asked casually, "Back to Sam's?"

Piper nodded. She hoped Phoebe's magic touch didn't tune into any more innocents in distress while she paid Sam for their abandoned fruits and vegetables. One more rescue and her sour cream would turn to spoiled sour soup in the midday heat.

Waiting for the light to change again, Phoebe cast a sidelong glance at Piper. "So just how tall, how tan, and how hot is Rick on a scale of one to ten?"

Phoebe dropped a bag of groceries on the counter and sighed, glad to be home. She had stayed in the car while Piper finished her business with Sam. Although Phoebe hadn't said anything, she had developed a slight headache. Going shopping had put a dent in her lazy day, but she hadn't bargained on running a rescue marathon that left her feeling as if *she* had been hit by a truck.

"Where's Prue?" Piper dropped the last bag on the table and opened the refrigerator.

"Still in her darkroom, I guess." Phoebe began unloading her bag. She handed Piper everything that needed to be kept cold and tried to think of a good reason to bail on the "making" part of the snack fest. Aside from being exhausted after their multiple adventures, she didn't have Piper's culinary skills, even when no actual cooking was involved. Mixing magical potions was entirely different.

"You look beat." Piper cast a sidelong glance at Phoebe as she stuffed plastic grocery bags into a paper bag for recycling.

"I am a little tired," Phoebe admitted. "Do you mind if I beg off making black bread squares? Mine will probably come out looking more like trapezoids anyway."

"Trapezoids would be interesting," Piper teased, "but I can manage without you."

"You sure?" Phoebe gave Piper three containers of cream cheese and sank into a kitchen chair.

"Positive." Piper stuffed the cream cheese in the fridge, then picked up the kettle. "Want some tea?"

Phoebe nodded. A soothing cup of tea, aspirin, and a nap might cure the headache. Dropping her chin on her folded arms, she glanced to the side when Prue came out of the darkroom. She looked upset.

Piper turned on the kettle and eased into a chair

when Prue sat down. "You look like I feel when I ruin a soufflé, Prue. Didn't your shots of Tremaine come out?"

"Most of them did." Exhaling, Prue spread the photos on the table.

"Gee, Stephen Tremaine looks just like our couch." Phoebe raised an eyebrow. Why had Prue created a portrait gallery of the Halliwell furniture?

"This is good." Piper moved one of the shots closer. "You really captured the inner essence of the coffee table."

Prue playfully cuffed Piper's arm. "That wasn't the objective. I was testing the film and the lens for defects."

"Oh." Phoebe sat up to get a better look and frowned. "They look fine to me."

"I know." Prue's eyes narrowed with dismay. "That's the problem."

"It is?" Piper jumped up when the kettle whistled and took it off the burner.

"Yeah." Prue pulled a photo of Tremaine out from under the scattered pile.

"Great shot, Prue!" Phoebe nodded, impressed. The lighting and angle softened the hard lines of Tremaine's face. His expression seemed a bit befuddled, though. "What's that?" Phoebe pointed to the oval stone in Tremaine's hand.

"That's the problem." Prue took a cup of steaming tea from Piper, but her puzzled gaze remained on the picture.

"I can see why." Piper handed Phoebe a cup and sat down again. "How come he's holding a rock?"

"It's not a rock. Well, not exactly." Prue sipped her tea then set it aside. "According to Tremaine it's some kind of spirit stone from an ancient culture in South America. He said it's thousands of years old." She frowned again as she ran her finger over the image.

Curious, Phoebe pulled her glasses from the cloth bag she had dropped on the table and slipped them on. The wispy gray discoloration on the image instantly came into focus. "It's smudged or something."

"Yep." Prue's mouth set in a tight line.

"Bummer." Piper patted Prue's shoulder. "It was a great shot. I'm sure Tremaine would have loved it."

"That's not what I'm worried about." Prue hesitated, caught Phoebe and Piper's bewildered stares, and picked up the picture of the couch. "This shot is fine. This one isn't." She tapped the photo of Tremaine. "And I don't know why."

Piper stiffened, suddenly on edge. "And this is a problem because?"

"You have to go back and reshoot Tremaine?" Phoebe offered.

Prue shook her head. "There's nothing wrong with the lens. Could be a manufacturing defect in the film—or maybe it's something else."

Phoebe's heart skipped a beat. For the Charmed Ones, "something else" usually translated as "something bad," and that usually meant big, bad trouble.

So much for my nap, Phoebe thought with a weary sigh.

CHAPTER
6

The calm, studious atmosphere in the university library took the edge off Prue's frayed nerves as she followed Phoebe to a study table in a quiet corner. Her pulse was still racing from their mad dash across campus to save a student from being struck by a tree limb.

"I need to sit down." Phoebe slipped into a chair and rubbed her temples.

"Ditto that." Prue dropped her bag and the folder with the photos of Tremaine and the spirit stone on the table. "Are you sure you're okay?"

"Just a little headache. I'll be fine." Phoebe pulled the photos from the folder and smiled. "Go get those reference books so we can track this critter down."

Phoebe's smile did not reassure Prue, but she

decided to let it go until they got home. Finding out
if there was some unknown threat lurking below
the radar had to take precedence over minor dis-
comforts.

"This could be just a wild goose chase," Prue
said.

"Yeah, but at least we can do it sitting down."
Phoebe sighed.

"You sit. I'll be right back." Prue smiled to reassure her sister, but her own thoughts were troubled.

Prue had been astounded when Piper and
Phoebe had briefed her about their hectic and harrowing shopping trip. Phoebe sometimes went for
days without having a vision. This day she had had
five. It was, Prue realized, inevitable that Phoebe's
power would grow stronger, too. She just needed
some time to adjust to her increased sensitivity.

It wasn't going to be easy on Piper or her, either,
Prue thought as she scanned the anthropology and
archaeology book titles. Saving people from imminent disaster was always on their program, but they
might have to start making decisions on the merits
of each individual case.

Prue selected four books that dealt with early
South American cultures, then paused a moment to
reflect.

There was no way they could have ignored the
jogger who bumped into Phoebe near the student
parking lot. Phoebe's power to divert the falling
tree limb had saved the young man from a broken
neck. Paper cuts, on the other hand, did not warrant
Charmed attention. The sisters simply couldn't risk

missing a major event for anything that wasn't life threatening.

A blast of cold air sent a chill cascading down Prue's spine. Clutching the books, she fled the frigid draft and hurried back to Phoebe.

"So what have we got?" With her glasses perched on the bridge of her nose, Phoebe took a book. "*Lost Civilizations of the Amazon.* Sounds like a winner."

"Watch," Prue said as she sat down. "We'll find out that that stone is just a fancy ancient pestle or weight for a thatched roof."

"Much ado about nothing." Phoebe blew dust off the old text and flipped to the index. "That would be a pleasant change in the routine, wouldn't it?"

"Yes." Prue grinned. "And I'd get a perverse kick out of telling Mr. Stephen Tremaine his rare spirit stone was just an ordinary household utensil."

Phoebe peered at her over the rim of her glasses. "Do I detect a hint of interest?"

"I'm not that desperate." Prue shuddered but not at the thought of a romantic interlude with the wealthy, self-centered candidate. Another draft seemed to wrap her in a cold, invisible shroud. "I can't concentrate in this draft. You're a student here. Can you check these books out?"

"Sure." Phoebe frowned. "What draft?"

"The one from the air conditioning vent." Prue glanced upward and scanned the ceiling. No vents, at least not that she could see. She rubbed her arms, her frown deepening when the icy sensation passed, and quickly put a twinge of anxiety on hold. She couldn't let her imagination turn every little thing that didn't have an immediate, logical explanation into a potential problem of demonic proportions. She'd go nuts in a week. Maybe less.

"Come on." Prue stood up and gathered her things. "If we go home, I can do research in the comfort of our own photogenic couch and you can rest your aching head."

"Good plan." Phoebe slammed the book closed.

Outside, Prue welcomed the warmth of the afternoon sun on her face and arms as they headed back to the car. The sight of students wandering the campus paths or sitting in groups on the grass helped to dissipate the sense of gloom that had settled over her in the library. Somehow she had to take control of the paranoia that assumed evil lurked under every rock.

"Somebody dropped their purse organizer." Phoebe stooped to pick up the woman's wallet lying in the parking space beside their car. She went into a precognitive trance the instant her fingers touched leather.

Piper stirred the mixture of softened cream cheese, chopped scallions, and seasonings with a vengeance. Tears streamed down her cheeks, forcing her to stop to wipe them away with the back of her hand. After Phoebe and Prue had left for the university library, she had thought making the ham rolls would take her mind off missing Leo. Instead, the mundane activity had just made things worse.

Without her sisters or some impending calamity

to distract her, Piper's thoughts automatically shifted to the emptiness she felt when Leo wasn't around. Which was most of the time lately, she thought sniffling. She couldn't even listen to music on the radio without falling into the pit of self-pity. Every song, whether it was about love lost or found, reminded her that their relationship encompassed both.

Setting the bowl aside, Piper opened the fridge to get the sliced ham and closed it again when the phone rang. She brushed a renegade wisp of hair off her forehead and took a deep breath to quell the weepy evidence of her emotions as she answered.

"Piper! It's Phoebe. We've got another emergency."

"What's happening?" Piper gave her sister her full attention, her personal problems forgotten.

"A woman falling out of a window in an alley behind an old brick building. We have an address," Phoebe said frantically. "I just hope it's the right one."

"Where?" Piper scribbled down the address and fished her keys out of her bag.

"You're closer, Piper! If we're not too late already," Phoebe added. "Meet you there."

Piper was driving down the street before she remembered that the cream cheese filling for the ham rolls was sitting on the counter, but there was no going back. A life literally hung in the balance. Unless she or Prue were on the scene to break the girl's fall, the victim didn't stand a chance.

Four minutes and thirty seconds later, Piper

burned rubber off her tires as she squealed into a parking lot at the side of the run-down apartment building. An access alley ran along the back. Prue's car wasn't there.

"Guess it's up to me." Since seconds might be crucial, Piper leaped out of the car without shutting off the engine and bolted for the back of the building. She braced herself for the worst as she rounded the corner and lurched to a halt by a large overflowing metal trash bin.

The alley was riddled with potholes, and the area in back of the building looked like a dump. Flies, attracted by the stench, swarmed around garbage and litter spilling out of torn trash bags. Broken glass, flattened cans, and discarded junk were piled by the back door.

But there was no body smashed to a pulp on the pavement, Piper noticed with relief.

A high-pitched squeal drew Piper's gaze upward past rows of dirty windows. The building was five stories tall, but she couldn't pinpoint which floor the cry had come from until the girl shrieked again.

"That hurt, Bobby!"

Angered by the domestic dispute, Piper positioned herself to be ready to act no matter what window the woman came flying out of. She wished Prue and Phoebe would hurry up. She could freeze a falling body, but the woman would still be falling when the effect wore off—at the same deadly velocity without Prue's telekinetic power to slow the descent.

"Come on, guys," Piper muttered, flexing her fingers. She frowned, fuming.

"Don't do that!" The woman yelled again.

"What?" A man's voice mocked her. "Can't take a little . . . Linda! Look out!"

Linda's terrified scream mingled with the sound of breaking glass as she burst backward through a window on the fourth floor and started to fall. Piper froze the back of the building with Linda suspended halfway out the shattered window.

"Okay. Now what?" Piper glanced up and down the alley to make sure nobody was watching the spectacle, then glowered toward the parking lot. No Prue or Phoebe, either, she thought, shivering as a gust of chilly wind blew through her hair. She frowned, startled by the anomaly in the eighty-degree heat.

Her attention was diverted from the icy breeze by Linda's scream when the action resumed. Reacting instinctively, she froze everything again.

And gawked in disbelief.

Linda was still halfway out the window.

Piper stared at Bobby, who had clamped onto Linda's wrist and had just started to pull her back in.

False alarm? Piper blinked and threw up her hands in frustration dissolving the time stall she had created.

"Bobby!" Linda's shrill cry pierced the quiet alley.

"Don't worry, baby! I've got you!" Bobby's voice shook with fright.

Piper thought she saw the man's grip begin to slip and stopped time a third time. She jerked back when a pair of silver-framed eyeglasses came to a dead stop in front of her eyes. Phoebe and Prue raced around the corner of the building as she snatched the glasses from certain doom.

"Oh, good. We're not too late." Phoebe's hand shot to her chest in relief.

"In the nick of time," Piper said. She held up the glasses. "I saved these, Prue. You save the girl."

"I'm ready whenever you are." As Prue raised her hand, time rolled forward.

"Don't let go!" Linda begged Bobby.

"He's losing her!" Phoebe suddenly rose in the air.

Prue latched onto Phoebe's ankle as Bobby hauled Linda back inside the apartment and threw his arms around her.

"Oh, boy." Squeezing her eyes shut, Phoebe tried without success to lower herself to the ground.

Piper watched with a stunned sense that everything was totally out of control. Since Bobby would have managed to abort Linda's death dive without their help, they had dropped everything to rescue a pair of glasses. The Celebrity Charity Bazaar was two days away, and she had a dozen things to do before she went to P3 for the night. And now Phoebe, who *really* needed to master her new ability to levitate, was airborne in front of witnesses. "Get her down!" Piper snapped.

"I'm trying!" Prue's blue eyes flashed as she hauled Phoebe back to earth and clamped onto her arms to keep her anchored. "Are you cool now?"

Phoebe nodded and looked up with a frown. "She wasn't going to fall?"

"Apparently not," Piper said.

"But I saw her smash through the window," Phoebe insisted.

"She did smash through the window. She just didn't fall and go splat." Phoebe looked so upset that Piper didn't mention that she had left her cream cheese filling rotting on the kitchen counter to answer a false alarm. When Bobby appeared in the window to check the damage, she lashed out at him instead.

"Hey!" Hands on her hips and itching for a fight, Piper snapped at Linda's bully boyfriend. "Where do you get off beating up on a girl and pushing her out a window?"

"I could give him a taste of his own medicine," Prue offered, waving her hand.

"What are you talking about, lady?" Bobby put his arm around Linda when she appeared beside him. "I didn't push her."

"No, you've got it all wrong." Linda pressed closer to Bobby as she looked down. "He was teaching me kung fu and I tripped."

Feeling like a complete idiot, Piper heaved a heavy sigh and held up the eyeglasses. "I'll just leave these here."

"This, too," Phoebe said softly. With a sheepish shrug, she placed the wallet on the pavement by the glasses.

As they made a hasty departure, Piper cast a narrowed glance at her sisters. "We have to talk!"

Athulak sped through the canyons of the city listening to the idle words of the humans who hurried along the streets or huddled behind walls. He had quickly learned to appreciate the advantages of being wind. No barrier could bar him, and no human feared him or recognized his touch.

The witches sensed him, but they knew not his name nor his power. Like the hundred others whose carelessly uttered desires he had granted since his return, the seer did not know she had been cursed by the impulsive whim of her own words.

Or that when Tremaine's words freed his spirit from the stone, the events set in motion could not be undone.

Except by the magic of the three.

Still, Athulak was untroubled as he rode the air currents through a sunlit sky.

What the witches did not know, they could not stop.

CHAPTER
7

Absorbed in her reading, Prue absently picked up her cup and took a long swallow of coffee. The cold, bitter liquid was a jolt to her system. "Gross!" She gagged, shuddered, and set the cup down on the kitchen table with weary resignation.

"Any luck?" Phoebe shuffled in and yawned. She paused by the stove and opened the kettle to check the water level.

"Zilch, nada, not even a hint." Leaning back, Prue closed the book and shoved it aside. The pile of university references had yielded some fascinating information about ancient South American tribes, but not a clue about a carved stone that resembled the one in Stephen Tremaine's library.

"So maybe there's nothing to find out about that stone guy." Phoebe turned on the burner under the kettle, stretched then rubbed her neck. "If it is a guy and not a paperweight or something."

"Ancient South American cultures didn't use paper." Prue held out her cup. "Would you dump that?"

"Sure." Phoebe emptied the cup in the sink, then pulled a teabag out of a canister. "Want some?"

Prue shook her head and stared at the clouded photo she had taken of Tremaine. Maybe Phoebe was right and the artifact was just a crudely carved rock with nothing exceptional about it except its obscure origin and age. The film was the most likely reason for the flaws in the pictures, especially since the sisters hadn't been attacked by any ferocious warrior demons from the past. They had enough problems without worrying about threats that didn't exist.

Like the rising rate of rescues prompted by the sudden surge in Phoebe's premonitions, Prue thought with a guarded glance at her sister. Phoebe was leaning against the counter massaging her temples.

"Didn't you sleep?" Prue asked.

"Yeah, I did." Sinking into a chair, Phoebe yawned again. "My brain just isn't used to the extra wear and tear yet."

Prue nodded. Since Phoebe had gone to sleep as soon as they had gotten home that afternoon, she and Piper hadn't had a chance to discuss a very real problem their sister didn't seem to recognize. Putting their lives on hold to save people from mortal and demonic danger was a responsibility they all accepted without question. Throwing their lives into chaos a dozen times a day to prevent trivial accidents was another matter entirely. Phoebe had to learn to distinguish between the two, but that wasn't something Prue wanted to address on her own. The youngest Halliwell would be easier to convince with the persuasive power of two.

"Feeling rested enough for a little fun?" Prue mimicked the arm movements of a Flamenco dancer. "Hard Crackers is playing at P3 tonight."

"You want to go now?" Phoebe glanced at the clock. "It's almost eleven."

"Afraid you'll turn into a pumpkin at midnight?" Prue joked to cloak her concern.

"Well, I . . . okay." Phoebe nodded and averted her gaze for a second. She smiled when she looked back, but there was no mischievous sparkle in her eyes. "Why not?"

That's what Prue wanted to know. Phoebe, who was never shy about scouting the dating possibilities at Piper's club, really didn't want to go out. *That* seemed even more ominous than the foggy picture of Tremaine's spirit stone. It definitely demanded a family conference of three, she decided as Phoebe got up to turn off the stove.

Phoebe stared apprehensively at the mass of people waiting to get into the club. She usually didn't mind having to push her way inside because an overflow crowd meant Piper was making money and she could stay in school. Now, instead of chic, well-dressed dollar signs, every person represented a potential red alert. Pretending that she felt fine in spite of a persistent headache had been difficult in the unpopulated sanctuary of her own house. Braving a packed house at P3 could be a waking nightmare.

Phoebe was ashamed to admit it, but if anyone was on the verge of impending catastrophe tonight, she didn't want to know about it.

"Look at that crowd! Not bad for a week night." Prue eased out of the car and smoothed the skirt of a black dress that hugged every curve. A black lace cover-up with long, tapering sleeves that belled at the cuffs created an image of daring elegance.

Phoebe called it Prue's deadly black widow look; no guy who was still breathing could resist her. Prue, however, showed no mercy and rejected most of the poor souls with the courage to ask her out. That wasn't hard to understand. They all had to err on the side of caution because of their powers. Even if she herself hit it off with the new bartender Piper had been urging her to meet the past few days, Phoebe thought, eventually her secret life as a witch would create problems most guys couldn't handle. Being in love with a White Lighter wasn't easy, but at least Piper didn't have to hide what she was.

"That's a lot of people all right." Chilled by a gust of wind, Phoebe rubbed her bare arms. The vibrant colors in her long wraparound skirt and matching midriff top were hotter than the night air.

"Are you cold?" Prue asked.

"It's a little chilly, but I'll warm up once we get inside. All those bodies dancing in close quarters generate a lot of heat." Phoebe didn't know if Rick was working tonight, but she had dressed to impress just in case.

Prue's eyes narrowed in puzzlement. "It's hot out here."

"But I just felt—" Phoebe frowned, realizing Prue was right. It *was* hot.

"Felt what?" Prue stepped closer. "A blast of arctic wind out of nowhere?"

"Yeah." Phoebe looked at her quizzically. "Did you feel it, too?"

"Not just now, no," Prue said. "I felt a windy cold shoulder in the library this afternoon. Let's go see Piper."

Phoebe called Prue back when she started toward the crowd gathered around the front door. "Let's go in the back. We don't want to incite a riot because we can go to the head of the line."

"Good point." Prue did an about-face.

Not really, Phoebe thought as they entered through the back door into the storage area. She just hadn't decided how to tell her sisters she was suffering from premonition overload and didn't know if she could stand the constant and demanding responsibility. She had to come clean and soon, though, which was why she had agreed to come to P3 with Prue. If *The Book of Shadows* didn't contain a remedy, there wasn't a cure for a runaway power.

She didn't want to spend the rest of her life in her room or forsake her duty as a Charmed One, but she wouldn't be much good to anyone if she went mad.

Phoebe paused in the storage area doorway to

survey the crowded club. There wasn't a vacant
seat in the house, including the bar stools. Hard
Crackers was apparently on a break, but that didn't
deter the habitually energetic. The dance floor was
packed with couples gyrating to the music on the
band's promotional CD. Piper was washing glasses
while the bartenders, Jimmy Dougan and Monica
Reynolds, poured drinks.

Phoebe was more relieved than disappointed to
see Jimmy and the dark-haired, willowy Monica
instead of the blond, tan Rick behind the bar. The
run-amok visions had put a definitive crimp in her
easygoing style, and a new relationship wouldn't
have much of a chance until she had the problem
under control. Just holding hands to dance might
prompt a too-powerful premonition.

No one was sitting in the alcove on the back wall
because Piper had put up a reserved sign. Phoebe
assumed Piper had held the comfy couch for them
since Prue had called to say they were on their way.
She was silently grateful. The alcove was set so far
back she wouldn't have to worry about bumping
elbows with anyone.

After she got there.

"I'm going to go sit down!" Phoebe shouted at
Prue to be heard over the noise and motioned
toward the bar. "You get Piper!"

Nodding, Prue gave her a thumbs-up and
slipped into the throng like a knife cutting butter.
The sea of bodies separated and closed back around
her in a fluid movement as she passed.

"Now my turn." Taking a deep breath, Phoebe

eased along the wall hoping whoever she touched led a completely disaster-free existence. No such luck.

A heavyset guy wearing no-style-whatsoever baggy pants and a loose shirt leaned against the wall in front of her to block her path. "Hey, cute thing, I've been waiting for you."

"Funny, but no thanks. I'm meeting someone." Donning a perky smile, Phoebe edged by him. The vision hit like a lightning bolt.

. . . open refrigerator, plate of cold chicken . . . the man clawing at his throat, choking on a bone . . .

Phoebe stepped back and looked him in the eye. "When you get home, do *not* eat chicken."

"Chicken?" Startled, the man blinked, bewildered.

"The leftovers in your fridge." Phoebe didn't care if he thought she was a nut case as long as she made her point. "It's bad, rotten, spoiled chicken. Eat it and you die. Got it?"

Dumbfounded, the man just nodded.

"I'm not kidding," Phoebe added as she pushed past him. She immediately brushed against a young woman who was staring into space and fighting back tears. The woman's lower lip trembled as she raised her glass and downed her drink.

. . . stopped by a cop, too drunk to stand without wobbling, arrested . . .

Rocked by the second vision, Phoebe couldn't move for a moment. Pressed between the woman, who was drowning her sorrows over a broken love affair, and a man who would stub his toe on his way to bed, she struggled for control. When the disorientation passed, she moved back to the wall and flattened herself against it.

With her stomach in knots and her head throbbing, Phoebe took her time and reached the alcove without another close encounter. Settling down on the couch, she made a mental note to tell Piper that the heartbroken woman would need to take a cab home. She took comfort in knowing she had kept two more lives from being ruined, but that didn't solve her problem.

When Piper and Phoebe arrived a few minutes later, Phoebe's stomach had started to relax and the pounding in her head had diminished. Even so, she must have looked terrible.

"What happened?" Piper exclaimed, sitting down beside her. "You're shaking."

"And white as a sheet." Prue placed her hand on Phoebe's forehead. "No fever."

"I'm not sick," Phoebe said. "It's worse."

Composing herself, Phoebe filled them in on the escalating number of visions and the debilitating effects, physical, emotional, and mental. She was near tears herself when she confessed that she wasn't sure she could take it.

"And we were worried about responding to endless false alarms." Piper gently brushed Phoebe's hair back from her face. "I didn't stop to think how hard this might be on you."

"Me, either." Prue gripped Phoebe's hand. "I was too busy worrying about an old stone that turned out to be just an old stone."

"Are you sure about that?" Piper asked.

"Pretty sure." Prue shrugged. "I mean, nothing strange has happened."

"Except that Phoebe's suddenly a walking code blue lightning rod," Piper said. "My power got stronger gradually, not all at once."

"True, but I discovered my ability to astral project instantly." Prue frowned. "The telekinesis got stronger gradually."

"The cold wind thing was sort of strange." Phoebe was relieved now that her sisters knew she was having trouble with her increased sensitivity. Still, if there was any chance that her enhanced power wasn't a natural occurrence, she really wanted to know. Before, she had connected only with desperate people who were threatened by demons and other evil entities with lethal intent. Being oversensitive could prevent her from getting the mental messages she was supposed to receive.

Piper tensed. "You mean like a gust of ice-cold air that shouldn't be there on a hot afternoon?"

"You felt it, too?" Prue stared at Piper intently.

"Today when I wasn't saving Linda." Piper's worried expression changed to one of curious puzzlement when she glanced toward the bar. "Oh, my."

Phoebe looked up to see a tall, muscular man with thick sandy blond hair and a killer tan moving through the crowd. Her breath caught in her throat when he stopped before them, shoved his hands in his pockets and smiled. Dimples and perfect white teeth, she noted.

"Hi, Piper," the man said.

Deep, husky voice and a twinkle in green eyes flecked with amber, Phoebe thought, continuing her inventory.

"How's it going, Rick?" Piper struggled to control a grin when Phoebe stiffened with surprise.

Prue cocked an eyebrow and subtly nodded her approval.

"Great." Rick smiled at Phoebe, holding her stunned gaze for a moment before turning back to Piper. "Monica said you were looking for more help to set up your booth at the charity bazaar on Saturday, and I'm available."

"So am I." Phoebe quickly qualified the remark. "To work on the P3 booth, I mean. This Saturday."

"The fringe benefits of working for your sister." Rick's smile widened as he looked into Phoebe's dark eyes again.

"Be here at seven Saturday morning," Piper said. "We'll be arriving at the park separately, but Jimmy will let you know what to do."

"I'll be here." Rick started to back off, then turned toward Phoebe. "I'll see you Saturday."

"You most certainly will." Phoebe was caught completely off guard when he suddenly lifted her hand and kissed it. The images that flooded her mind masked what happened next in real time.

. . . *Rick raising a fist to defend himself, attacked from behind, a club crashing down on his head . . . blood gushing from his smashed skull . . .*

"Come on, Phoebe." Prue's anxious voice broke through the fog that muddled Phoebe's mind, but

she couldn't shake off the physical effects for several more crucial seconds.

"Where's Rick?" Phoebe finally managed to
whisper. Sharp pains arrowed through her brain
and ricocheted off the inside of her skull. Shaky and
nauseous, she breathed in and out deeply to quell
the sensations. Apparently, her system reacted in
direct proportion to the intensity of the violence in
the disasters she foresaw.

"He just left," Piper said, scanning the crowd.

"He gets mugged in the alley." Phoebe's eyes
widened with horror. "They're going to kill him."

"No, they won't." Prue jumped up. "You stay
here. We'll take care of it."

Phoebe grabbed Piper's wrist. "Don't do anything we can't explain. About us . . ."

"We'll handle it." Piper squeezed Phoebe's hand,
then shoved through the crowd after Prue.

Feeling sick and disoriented, Phoebe pulled herself up and pulled herself together. Rick hadn't
worked for Piper very long. Still, Phoebe realized,
her sister had intuitively recognized that she and
Rick would connect. For a while or forever, the
immediate rapport had been there. She couldn't just
sit while her sisters tried to stop a gang of street
thugs from bashing in Rick's brains.

Hugging the wall again, Phoebe worked her way
to the storage area door. Her progress was ham-
pered only by a fleeting vision of an awkward nerd
slamming his fingers in his car door. He'd survive.
She pressed on, driven by the need to know that
Rick would, too.

Phoebe found Piper and Prue watching the brawl from the shadows of the exterior doorway. Prue glanced at her with disapproval, then quickly turned her attention back to the alley. Rick was managing to block and strike back at a burly unarmed teenager while keeping an eye on the two other boys as they moved to flank him. When Rick smashed his fist into the burly kid's jaw throwing him off his feet, the boy on his right charged with a knife.

Phoebe didn't question why Piper and Prue were letting the fight play out. Knowing that she wanted to get to know Rick better, they were waiting until the critical moment before they intervened in the hope that they could save him without revealing themselves.

Phoebe's heart leaped into her throat as Rick's hand clamped around the boy's wrist, staying the blade's downward plunge. With practiced precision, he swung his leg to knock the attacker's legs out from under him. As the second boy fell, Rick swung to face the first boy, who staggered back with his fist raised. Behind Rick, the third boy picked up a broken table leg that had fallen out of the P3 dumpster.

"Get it!" Phoebe whispered in Prue's ear.

Prue acted instantly. With a targeted flick of her finger, she telekinetically seized the table leg, yanked it out of the boy's hand, and heaved it onto the roof, out of reach.

Stunned, the third boy jerked to a halt.

Since his back was turned, Rick did not know why the boy behind him suddenly panicked and

took off down the alley toward the street. Already
beaten by Rick's superior fighting skills, the other
two ruffians turned tail and ran after him. Exhaling,
Rick bent over to catch his breath.

Prue, Piper, and Phoebe eased back from the
doorway and ducked into the storage room.

"Thanks." Phoebe leaned against the wall to
steady herself. Her pulse was still racing, and the
pains in her head had subsided to a dull but tor-
menting throb.

"No problem. At least, not with Rick."
Smoothing her hair back, Piper turned to Prue. "I
don't think it would hurt to dig a little deeper into
ancient tribal cultures of South America. Cold
winds in August might have a scientific explanation, but it can't possibly be coincidence that we all
felt one at different times in different locations."

Prue nodded. "I don't know much about spirit
stones, but assuming they were used as receptacles
to bind spirits—"

"—maybe one got loose," Piper finished. "The
question is which one and why? And what does it
want?"

"Professor Rubin in the anthropology department at the university might be able to help,"
Phoebe suggested. "I've never met him, but I've
heard he's a little eccentric. He's written a few
books about early cultures, though."

"Why didn't you say so today when we were
there?" Prue asked, looking a bit perturbed.

"Because he's a joke around campus." Phoebe
made a circling gesture around her ear. "Apparently,

Professor Rubin didn't go off the deep end until *after* they gave him tenure. Besides, this afternoon I didn't really think we had a problem."

"I'll go see him tomorrow after I drop my Tremaine shots off at *415.*" Prue didn't look convinced that the effort would be worth the trip. "Can you give me directions to his office?"

"Better. I'll take you there," Phoebe said.

"No!" Piper objected. "You're confined to quarters until we figure this thing out. No leaving the house."

"Don't even answer the door," Prue added.

"But—" Phoebe started to protest, then realized Piper and Prue were right. If they did have an unidentified demon problem, they couldn't afford to waste time and energy rescuing people from fender benders and bee stings.

CHAPTER
8

Dr. Gregory Rubin's office was in the basement of
the cultural sciences building. Prue walked down
the dim corridor with Phoebe's directions clutched
in her hand, a photo of the spirit stone in her bag,
and a nagging sense that she was wasting her time.

For one thing, the professor's subterranean
domain was obviously not a maintenance priority.
Paint was peeling off gray walls, and several wire
light fixtures had burned-out or missing bulbs.
Condensation from overhead air conditioning ducts
dripped, forming small puddles on the floor, and
water pipes rattled. Since the administration
couldn't fire the tenured professor for being a kook
as long as he did his job, they had, apparently, ban-
ished him to the basement, hoping he would quit.

The dismal surroundings didn't instill Prue with

confidence that the research trip would be worth the effort. However, since she had come this far she might as well follow through. Eccentric academics were often brilliant.

"I can hope," Prue muttered as she stopped before a solid door with Prof. Rubin stenciled in black on gray. A bulletin board hanging on the wall beside the door caught her eye as she started to knock. She skimmed over the class schedules and seminar flyers to a faded book jacket that was curling at the corners: *Ancient Cults of the New World* by Dr. Gregory Rubin. A yellowed newspaper review was tacked up beside it. The book had made the nonfiction bestseller list twenty-seven years earlier.

Phoebe hadn't mentioned that Rubin was an expert on cults, but the knowledge boosted Prue's hopes. Quite possibly, his reputation for being unhinged stemmed from an academic prejudice against anything related to the supernatural.

As Prue raised her fist to knock, the door was thrown open from the inside. A stoop-shouldered, elderly man wearing a crumpled brimmed hat, a wrinkled suit with a loosened tie, and wire-rimmed glasses looked up from the papers in his hand. Startled to see her, he gasped and staggered backward.

Afraid the old man might have a heart attack on the spot, Prue quickly moved to steady him. "I'm so sorry, Professor Rubin. Are you all right?"

"I'm too old to be all right," the professor grumbled. "And according to my esteemed colleagues, I'm too daft to *be* right . . . about anything. Now, if you'll unhand me—"

Prue let go of his arm. "Sorry again."

"So am I. That I'm not forty years younger." He winked, disarming and charming Prue. "Now, what's a pretty girl like you doing wandering around down here? Are you lost?"

"No, I came to see you." Prue pulled the photograph out of her bag. "About this."

The old man took the photo and squinted through his glasses as he studied it. "Why would you be asking me about Stephen Tremaine? I detest the man."

"You do?" Prue wasn't sure what to say. She didn't want to offend the old guy.

"Most definitely!" Rubin's eyes flashed with anger. "Tremaine may have the finest private collection of primitive artifacts in the world, but he doesn't give a hoot about their cultural or historical significance. The man is contemptibly incurious."

They were on the same page there, Prue thought.

Rubin shoved the picture back at her. "You can forget about asking me to vote for this scoundrel. I won't support someone who's more interested in lining his friends' pockets than protecting our endangered environment."

"I'm not campaigning for Tremaine, Professor Rubin. I want to know about this." Prue pointed to the artifact in Tremaine's hand.

Rubin tilted his head back and squinted at the photo again. "Oh, I see. Interesting."

Taking the picture, the professor wandered over to a desk that was piled high with books, notebooks, file folders, empty fast food containers, and various office items including a banker's lamp with a green glass shade. He settled into a desk chair, took off his hat and dropped it on the floor, then picked up a magnifying glass. The old chair squeaked as he leaned back to examine the photo more closely.

Prue took a moment to look around the office, which more closely resembled a combination warehouse, museum, and library. Gray metal shelves covering most of the wall space were stuffed with books, rolled charts, and artifacts. The overflow was stacked or scattered on the floor. The old man's definition of filing was just to get the folders in the vicinity of the filing cabinets, she surmised. Several folders were jammed into open drawers while others were piled on top of or around the old metal cabinets. Packing crates, opened and unopened, stood along the far wall by two huge workbenches. She found herself wondering if, perhaps, the professor *liked* being in the basement where no one would complain about his functional disorganization.

"Do you know where Tremaine acquired this?" the professor asked.

"South America somewhere." Prue perched on a dusty chair opposite the desk. "He said it might be a spirit stone and that it was over three thousand years old."

The old man grunted. "Remarkably astute of him, although I hate having to admit it." Setting the magnifying glass down, he peered at Prue intently. "So what is it you need from me, then?"

Prue was blunt to save time. "I want to know if

it's possible for a spirit to escape one of these stones, and if so—who or what might have occupied this one?"

The old man's penetrating gaze stayed fixed on her, but she didn't blink or look away. "Such things are nonsense," he said finally. "The superstitions of ignorant people needing something or someone more powerful than they to blame for misfortune and natural disaster over which they had no control."

"Perhaps," Prue countered. "But I've always found it fascinating that so many ancient beliefs were shared by cultures that never had contact with each other. Too many similar myths to be explained as mere coincidence, don't you think?"

"Perhaps." The old man paused. "You're not pulling my leg, are you?"

"No, sir, I'm not." Prue wasn't sure if Rubin thought she was slightly unhinged or whether he was surprised to find a believer. As she and her sisters had found out, cult superstitions often had a basis in terrible, violent reality. Although mysticism and metaphysics were accepted in pop culture, the hallowed halls of many respected universities regarded such studies and theories as poppycock, to paraphrase Grams.

Sighing, the professor clasped his hands on his stomach. "You do understand that an academic who gave credence to such a preposterous theory could be forced into retirement. The income gained from museums seeking authentication of their new acquisitions would not offset the ridicule."

"Perfectly." Prue smiled to assure him she understood that whatever he told her was just between them. He was well past retirement age. His expertise and his scientific reputation were his job security, and she had the feeling he had come close to forced unemployment in the past.

The old man nodded and adjusted his glasses to glance at the photo again. "There are legends, an oral history that's told among certain tribes who still live in the jungles of the Amazon. I suspect that stone represents Athulak, an entity in human form who created and thrived on chaos."

"Sounds like some people I've known," Prue quipped.

"Yes, me, too, I'm sorry to say." Grinning, he relaxed and continued. "As the story goes, Athulak could twist the intent of prayers for peace and prosperity to bring disaster instead. The tribe prayed for rain and got devastating floods. They asked for game and were overrun with disease-ridden pests. You get the idea."

"Yes, I do." Prue nodded, even though she couldn't make a connection between the legend and current events. "How did Athulak get into the stone?"

"Assuming that is the stone, which I doubt," the professor clarified, "he was imprisoned by a powerful woman who could manipulate the elements."

A witch, Prue thought.

"After Athulak was trapped, she buried the stone so a prayer with the potential to create irreversible, catastrophic mayhem could not release him."

"What makes you think this figure is Athulak?"
Prue asked, remembering that Tremaine had said
the stone was the only one of its kind in the world.

"The smooth contours and almost total lack of
detail," Rubin explained. "It's described in the stories. The symbolic order inherent in the shape and
design strengthened the power of the woman's
binding spell."

"Makes sense to me." Prue stuffed the photo
back in her purse and thanked the old man. Now
that she had a name, she could check *The Book of
Shadows.* She looked back when she reached the
door. "One more question, if you don't mind."

"Not at all." The professor leaned forward expec-
tantly.

"Could a disembodied spirit take form as a cold
gust of wind?"

The old man hesitated, rubbing his chin, then
shrugged. "I don't have the foggiest. An interesting
theory, however, if one believes in spirits."

"What did you find out?" Phoebe turned *Dark
Passions at Midnight* facedown on the coffee table
when Prue came in. A good night's sleep and a day
without visions had cured her headache, and she
had finally gotten a few lazy hours of downtime to
read. She had enjoyed herself, but she didn't want
to spend the rest of her life as a hermit doing nothing because her power was out of control.

Prue glanced at the paperback cover. "Doing
some heavy reading to take your mind off your
troubles?"

"Compared to Agatha Cross and Trevor Holcombe, my life is boring." Phoebe wasn't about to admit she was enjoying the steamy novel, made steamier by substituting Rick and herself as the hero and heroine. There were some secrets sisters did not have to share. "So how was Professor Rubin? As creepy and cantankerous as they say?"

"More like sweet and lovable—for a wizened, cranky old man," Prue said. "And very helpful. I think."

"You think?" Phoebe sagged. "I was hoping for something a little more definitive."

"Well, maybe you and Piper will think of something I didn't." Prue glanced toward the kitchen. "Is she back from P3, yet? I'd rather explain this only once."

Phoebe shook her head. Piper had taken Prue's photos of P3 and the other things she had gathered to decorate the bazaar booth to the club. She also had to check with the rental company to make sure the small fridge would be delivered to the park on time. If all went according to plan in the morning, Rick and the rest of the setup crew would have everything ready to go by the time the wholesaler arrived with the food and beverages.

"She's getting a little tense and testy about the bazaar tomorrow," Phoebe said. "So I really hope you don't have bad news."

They both looked toward the front hall when the door opened and slammed closed.

Piper stomped in looking furious. "Do you have any idea how much it costs to rent a refrigerator for a day?"

"Not a clue," Phoebe said.

"How much?" Prue asked.

"Too much. So I bought one instead, but it's a write-off," Piper added quickly. "I can use it in the storeroom at the club." As she started to sit, Prue grabbed her arm and pulled her back up.

"Before you get comfy, we have to check *The Book of Shadows*." Prue hauled Piper into the hall and glanced back at Phoebe. "Coming?"

"Right behind you." Phoebe finished the ginger ale in her glass and hurried to catch up.

"Check for what?" Piper asked as they trooped up the stairs to the attic.

"An entity called Athulak," Prue explained. "He had a thing for chaos. According to the legends and Professor Rubin, a witch bound him in the stone and buried it. I think Tremaine's archaeological expedition dug him up."

Prue dropped her bag by Grams's old rocker and went to the pedestal that held *The Book of Shadows*.

Phoebe sank into the old rocker, taking comfort from the Halliwell history that was stored in the attic. Family heirlooms from centuries ago to the dress she had worn to her high school prom had all been lovingly saved. Most important, however, was the leather-bound *Book of Shadows*, which had unlocked to reveal the magical secrets of their ancestors when their own powers had been awakened. New spells and information were added as needed when Grams or another long-dead relative had them to give.

"Does he have anything to do with my visions?"

Phoebe crossed her fingers as Prue flipped the pages.

Prue looked up from the book with a frown. "Have you said any prayers for peace and prosperity lately?"

"Not since last Christmas," Phoebe said. "Peace on earth, goodwill to men and all."

"I don't think that's what Prue meant." Piper sat on an old beanbag chair that had lost its poof and clutched a dingy old throw pillow to her chest. "What did you mean?" she asked Prue.

"Professor Rubin said Athulak had the power to corrupt the people's prayers so they created disaster instead of peace and prosperity. Pray for rain, get floods. That kind of thing," Prue explained and continued turning the pages.

Phoebe rocked, which helped her think. "I don't think that applies to me."

"Why not?" Piper cocked her head, puzzled.

"Because being able to connect with more people has helped us *avert* disaster, not create it." Discouraged, Phoebe stopped rocking. Planting her elbows on her knees, she rested her chin in her hands.

"Good point." Sighing, Piper turned back to Prue. "Anything?"

Prue shook her head and stood back. "Not yet, anyway."

Phoebe stared at the book. Occasionally, an invisible ancestor's spirit would open the book to the right reference for them. The pages didn't even ruffle as the seconds passed.

"I guess we don't get any help this time." Piper sighed.

Depressed, Phoebe hung her head. She desperately wanted something external to be responsible for her new, precognitive ultrasensitivity, but wanting something didn't make it so. Or did it? Her brain suddenly shifted into high gear.

"Brainstorm!" Phoebe flew out of the chair, her gaze snapping from one sister's perplexed face to the other. "Don't people usually pray because they *want* something?"

"Or because they're grateful for something," Piper said.

Phoebe rolled her eyes, then started to pace to collect her thoughts. She knew she was grasping at straws, but they didn't have anything else. "Well, isn't a wish the same thing?"

Prue frowned.

Piper blinked.

"Yesterday morning when I was watching the news," Phoebe reminded them, "I *wished* that my power was stronger so I could help more people and—bingo! My power is stronger."

"Possible?" Piper looked at Prue.

"Theoretically." Prue's frown deepened as she moved to her bag and removed the photo.

Phoebe looked over Prue's shoulder at the gray smoky flaw that obstructed the image of the spirit stone. "What?"

"I'm not sure." Prue stared at the photo, her brow wrinkled and her eyes narrowed in thought. Piper and Phoebe both tensed when she inhaled sharply and her blue eyes widened with an unknown revelation. "This meeting is adjourned to the kitchen."

"Why?" Phoebe tried, but she couldn't quell a rush of excitement. "What?"

"I don't want to get your hopes up." Prue ran for the door. "I have to check something first!"

"What?" Phoebe called after her. "I can take it! Honest!" She stamped her foot as Prue disappeared down the stairs and glared at the open door.

"How about a few ham rolls while we wait." Piper draped an arm over Phoebe's shoulders. "I made up a double batch of black bread and cream cheese squares, too."

Piper's offer calmed Phoebe's stressed nerves. However, she couldn't accept without confessing. "I, uh, already taste tested a few . . . several, actually. Maybe a dozen."

"No biggie," Piper teased. "I calculated in the Phoebe snitch factor when I made them. Besides, it doesn't look like Leo's going to show up any time soon to eat them."

Letting Piper go ahead, Phoebe paused to switch off the attic light. Her thoughts and emotions were in turmoil wondering what Prue was checking into. She didn't want a showdown with a nasty spirit, but the alternative was worse.

She would be condemned to the torture of endless brushes with everyone else's disasters or the torment of complete, unending isolation.

CHAPTER
9

Where is she?" Phoebe stood with her hands on her hips and a look of consternation on her face.

Piper pulled a plate of black bread squares out of the refrigerator and stuffed one in Phoebe's mouth. "Chew and chill."

Phoebe scowled, pushed the snack into her mouth, and grabbed another off the plate before Piper set it on the counter.

Inhaling and exhaling with quiet frustration, Piper reached into the refrigerator for a tray of ham rolls and began to slice them into circular bite-size pieces. She didn't mean to appear insensitive to Phoebe, but if Prue didn't find any answers the disappointment would be worse. And it wasn't as though she didn't have her own problems. The Celebrity Charity Bazaar was costing more than she had anticipated. If the P3 booth didn't attract more business to the club, her PR budget for the year would be blown.

Stricken by a twinge of guilt, Piper stole a sidelong glance at Phoebe as she arranged the bread squares and ham rolls on a clean plate. Her younger sister was flipping through a magazine Prue had left on the table, but her outward calm didn't fool Piper. Being the early warning system for every cut, pimple, or fatal accident in the immediate future of every person she met was a difficult, if not impossible, burden to bear.

Prue emerged from the darkroom as Piper finished filling a bowl with fresh raw carrot sticks, broccoli, and cauliflower and set it on the table with a side of creamy dip.

"Take a look at these." Prue lined up four of the Tremaine photos in front of Phoebe.

Piper moved behind Phoebe and looked at the series of pictures one by one. "What are we looking for?"

"The pattern." Prue brushed her hair behind her ear, then pointed to the flaw over the spirit stone in each shot. "Every time I've looked at these shots in the order they were taken, I've had the feeling I was missing something. Now it's so obvious I can't believe it took me this long to figure it out. Don't you see it?"

"No," Piper answered honestly.

"I do," Phoebe said softly. "The blemish gets bigger in each shot."

"Yep, but that's not all." Prue ran her finger

across the glossies. "The origin point of the flaw is the same in each shot, too. It starts at the inside corner of the left eye."

Piper moved beside Phoebe to study the photos again. As Prue had pointed out, the gray shadow appeared to be elongating from the carved eye. Interesting but not conclusive, she thought warily. She tended to be as skeptical as Prue was quick to attribute everything bad that happened to an evil force. "I don't want to put a damper on your theory, Prue, but the images would be in the same spot in every picture if you used a damaged roll of film."

"Except they're not *exactly* in the same spot." Prue pulled a six-inch ruler out of her back pocket and measured the distance from the corner of the eye to the edge of every photo. The measurements were different and off by as much as an inch. "If the problem was the *film*, the flaw would be exactly two inches in from the side in every proof. They aren't. The flaw originates in the eye in every photo regardless of the angle."

"Is this a eureka moment?" Phoebe asked hesitantly.

"I think so. My camera captured the essence of Athulak escaping the stone." Prue grinned, immensely pleased with herself.

"Woohoo!" Phoebe raised her hand to high-five with Prue, then threw her arms around Prue's waist and hugged her. "What a relief!"

"Wait a minute!" Piper held up her hands. "Having an ancient spirit who causes chaos on the loose is *not* a reason to celebrate."

"Oh, right." Prue immediately stopped smiling and coughed.

"I beg to differ," Phoebe said. "If Athulak made my power go berserk, then we can probably reverse his action."

"That's possible, but we really don't know much about him or how he operates." Piper pulled out a chair and sat down. "Assuming it's Athulak and not some other dastardly spirit with a completely different game plan that escaped Tremaine's rock."

"Okay, okay." Prue sat down on the other side of Phoebe. "I admit we're assuming a lot, but we may know more than we think we do."

"Like what?" Piper wanted Prue's theory to be right as much as Phoebe did, but she wanted more proof than a few photos that *might* be flawed because of bad film.

"I'm not sure." Prue shrugged.

"Did Professor Rubin say anything else that might help us?" Phoebe asked Prue, then glanced at Piper. "I mean, let's just assume we're dealing with Athulak since we don't have any other likely suspects, okay?"

"Okay." Piper folded her arms and crossed her legs. When she issued a challenge, Prue and Phoebe usually took the bait and argued a convincing case. Right now Piper really wanted to be convinced. "For the sake of argument."

"Okay." The intensity of Phoebe's anxiety was evident in her hushed voice and probing stare as she leaned across the table. "What happened in

Tremaine's library, Prue? You or he must have done
something to break the binding spell."

"Well, let's see." Prue picked up a black bread
square and nibbled it while she thought. "Professor
Rubin said that after the witch trapped the spirit of
Athulak in the stone, she buried it so—" Prue paused,
apparently trying to remember the professor's exact
words. "So a prayer that could produce irreversible,
catastrophic mayhem couldn't set him free."

Piper recoiled slightly. "What did Tremaine do?
Pray for the end of the world?"

"No, he *wished* that he didn't have to run against
Noel Jefferson." Prue tapped the first photo in the
series of four on the table. "Just as I took this.
There's no flaw in the shots I snapped *before* he
made the wish."

"There you are!" Beaming with triumph, Phoebe
straightened and slapped her hands on the table.

Prue's satisfied smile segued into an irritated
frown when she noticed Piper's expression didn't
mirror her and Phoebe's elation. "What?" Prue
demanded. "Everything we've discussed falls right
into place with what's happened to Phoebe."

"Yes, as long as we ignore the fact that our powers got stronger without any outside interference,"
Piper responded.

"What about the cold winds?" Phoebe's eyes
flashed. "How do you explain that, Piper?"

"A cold wind that touched each of us at different
times," Prue added emphatically.

"And different locations." Phoebe lifted her chin,
defying Piper to argue.

"Four times." Piper slapped her forehead. "I felt the same frigid blast of cold air in the park!"

"When the pony ran amok?" Prue asked.

"Oh, boy." Phoebe closed her eyes for a second. "The pony went wild right after that little girl wished she *had* a pony."

"Apparently, Athulak delivered," Prue said.

"Except we stopped the disaster part." Phoebe popped a ham roll in her mouth.

"Which begs the question—" Piper shrugged when her sisters turned in tandem to stare. "What was Athulak doing at the park? Or in our living room?"

"When I opened my big mouth and wished myself into this mess," Phoebe mumbled.

Prue winced. "That's probably my fault. I, uh, used my power to stop the stone from falling over when Tremaine put it back in the display case."

Piper connected the rest of the dots. "Athulak saw you, and since he was imprisoned by a witch three thousand years ago, he decided to follow you to make sure it didn't happen again."

"I think that about covers it." Prue went to the refrigerator and removed a pitcher of orange juice. "Except I'm a little fuzzy on exactly where we're at or what we're supposed to do."

"Me, too." Phoebe scratched her head, puzzled. "I mean, Tremaine's wish doesn't sound like something that could cause irreparable harm to the world."

That part wasn't clear to Piper, either, but one indisputable fact was. "But it could spell big trouble for Noel Jefferson."

*   *   *

Athulak vented his fury on any humans in his
path as he followed the car carrying the witches. A
spear of concentrated wind speeding through the
city canyons at ground level, he stung bare flesh
with bitter cold and ripped packages out of grasping hands. Potted plants and plastic furniture, signs
and anything else that wasn't weighted down were
thrown about the streets in a frenzy of rage.

He took no pleasure in the panic his passing created and cursed the long-ago people that had carried the word of his defeat across the generations.

But his anger at the witches was greater and
fueled his hunger for vengeance.

Tenacious and blessed by the powers of good,
they had sensed him and gone in search of knowledge. He had foolishly believed the old witch had
buried his secrets with the stone.

Now the witches knew his name and his power,
and they were going to warn the focus of the primary wish.

He would not permit them to succeed.

When the car stopped by a large building,
Athulak waited until the witches got out. Then he
flattened and compressed the molecules of his
invisible but nonetheless physical, form. Honing
the edge of the molecular blade he had become, he
severed a tall metal pole and sliced a red, white,
and blue cloth to shreds as it drifted to the ground.

"Did you see that?" Phoebe paused halfway
across the parking lot outside the building that
housed the offices of the Public Defender.

Prue heard the flagpole snap and watched as Old Glory was ripped apart. There was only one plausible explanation. Athulak wasn't satisfied with making his presence known with cold kisses anymore. "Stick close to me and run!"

"It's Athulak, isn't it?" Phoebe pressed close to Prue as they charged for the door.

"That's my best guess." Concentrating, Prue swept her hand in a circle above her head, creating a constant telekinetic shield to ward off the invisible enemy. Until the flagpole had been snapped in half, she hadn't realized the wind spirit could cause them physical harm. She didn't stop when they burst through the door into the lobby. Athulak was a creature made of air, and he could infiltrate the securest building through the ventilation system.

"In there." Still waving her arm, Prue urged Phoebe into the rest room. The instant they were inside, she locked the door and stood on the counter to close the vent.

"What's going on?" Phoebe asked, her voice frantic.

"Apparently, Athulak can adjust his molecular density," Prue explained. "In other words, he can turn himself into a very sharp, very lethal, invisible sword."

"So why didn't he attack us before?"

Prue shrugged. "Maybe because we didn't know enough to be a threat before."

"That's not exactly comforting." Phoebe's hand went to her throat as her gaze shifted to the crack under the door. "What's to stop him from getting in under there?"

"Magic. You chant. I'll call Piper." Prue flipped open her cell phone. "We need a spell to protect us against a spirit wind."

"I'm no good at thinking up spells under pressure," Phoebe said frantically.

"Punt!" Prue dialed.

Nodding, Phoebe put her hand on the door and closed her eyes. "Fire, water, wind and air, cast in cosmic primal brine; bid Athulak's wind, beware! No passage through this door I bind."

When Piper answered, Prue quickly explained their new problem. "We need a charm, something we can carry to protect us from a spirit wind."

"I've seen a spell to ward off demons who take elemental form in *The Book of Shadows*," Piper said, "but it might take me a while to brew the potion and get there."

"We'll wait." Hanging up, Prue joined Phoebe, who was sitting on the counter, staring at the door. Once they had figured out that Noel Jefferson was in danger, they had realized they couldn't protect him unless they knew exactly what the danger was. Phoebe had volunteered to find out, even though touching him might be painful. The more violent the calamity, the harder the physical impact was on Phoebe.

And this time they were dealing with an event that might be the beginning of the end of the world.

Prue glanced at the door and smiled. "Nice job."

"I was motivated by the mental image of being beheaded in the parking lot." Phoebe shuddered.

Prue leaned back with a weary sigh. They had faced many demons, warlocks, and other malicious beings that had seemed too powerful to beat at first. They had always prevailed, but Athulak was unlike anything they had encountered before. They didn't have a clue how to vanquish him, and if Piper's protection charm didn't repel him, they had no defense against a razor-sharp molecular blade.

Prue tensed when she heard the murmur of voices and laughter in the hall outside. Someone tried to open the locked door and pounded when it wouldn't budge.

"Hey!" a female voice protested. "Open up!"

"Don't think so," Phoebe whispered, frowning.

Prue held up one hand to telekinetically reinforce the deadbolt and checked her watch. It was just after five. She hoped Piper showed up before a maintenance crew arrived to unlock the door or before everyone, including Noel Jefferson, went home.

Athulak had not been prepared for the destructive effects when he tried to cut through the witch's barrier. The impact with the undulating wall of force had almost annihilated his cohesion. In danger of having his molecules scattered on the lesser wind, he had mustered the last of his dwindling energy and retreated into the labyrinth of ducts in the building. He barely managed to hold himself together as he slipped through the tunnels and into the room where Noel Jefferson sat behind a desk.

Struggling to maintain his physical integrity, Athulak eased himself under the door of a smaller, dark room where the man kept many boxes and cloth coverings. Safe in the cramped space on the floor, Athulak relaxed and allowed himself to drift.

Thwarted and weakened, he rested to recoup his strength and nursed his hatred for the females and their overwhelming magic. He took comfort in knowing that soon the power of destruction would be his and found solace in the inevitability of his victory. No power on earth or beyond would be able to vanquish him or undo the cataclysm after the primary wish was fulfilled.

The chain of events begun when Tremaine had prayed to be delivered from his foe could not be stopped.

Unless the seer touched Jefferson and saw his destiny.

Athulak watched and waited. If necessary, he would risk further depletion of his diminished energies to strike the witches down.

CHAPTER
10

Startled awake when Piper knocked on the rest room door, Phoebe hit the back of her head on the mirror. She rubbed the spot as Prue unlocked the door.

"Sleeping on the job, guys?" Piper quipped as she entered.

"We didn't have a deck of cards to help pass the time," Phoebe retorted, rubbing her head. Actually, she couldn't believe she had dozed off with the slice-and-dice wind demon on the rampage. Spells composed on the spot in emergency situations didn't always perform as expected. Fortunately, her binding spell to keep the spirit wind out of the rest room had worked. Neither she nor Prue had lost any fingers or toes.

But she hadn't solved the problem that had

plagued her thoughts before she had drifted off.
They were so worried about protecting Noel
Jefferson, they hadn't addressed the possibility that
a wish Athulak granted might be permanent.
Runaway ponies and other single-occurrence disasters could be stopped, but what if the wish that had
enhanced her powers couldn't be reversed?

"What took you so long, Piper?" Prue slid off the
counter and took the leather-wrapped packet Piper
was holding out. "It's after seven."

"It's Friday night, and the downtown traffic is
brutal," Piper explained as she handed a second
packet to Phoebe.

"Better late than not at all." Phoebe sniffed the
spicy tang wafting off the small leather pouch, surprised by the pleasant scent. It reminded her of
warm spiced cider and cinnamon. The last charm
Piper had tried had smelled like burned cow
manure laced with rotten garbage. "What's in it?"

"Raw chicken hearts, falcon feather, and assorted
fungi with some ordinary household spices." Piper
eyed Prue pointedly. "It had to simmer for an hour."

"You did great, Piper. Thanks." Prue stuffed the
packet in the front pocket of her jeans. "You didn't
happen to notice if Noel Jefferson is still in the
building, did you?"

"Because if we're too late to stop whatever's
going to happen to him, Athulak wins and the
world is toast." Phoebe eased off the counter and
pocketed her charm.

"I don't know," Piper said. "I came directly here
from the main entrance."

"Guess we'd better find out." Slinging her bag over her shoulder, Phoebe waved her sisters toward the door.

The lobby was deserted, but all the lights were on, giving Phoebe some hope that Noel Jefferson was working late. A quick check of the wall directory by the elevator revealed that Jefferson's office was on the third floor. However, when Prue pushed the elevator call button, nothing happened.

"You must need a key to use it after hours." Prue hit the metal door with her fist.

"Can I help you, ladies?" a man asked sharply.

Phoebe glanced over her shoulder at a large security guard walking toward them. Instead of smiling, she opted for a look of frantic desperation, which wasn't difficult because she *was* frantically desperate. "I hope so. We have to see Noel Jefferson right away. It's an emergency."

"Life and death," Piper added.

"Yeah?" The man's frown deepened when he stopped in front of them. His suspicious gaze sized each of them up as though they matched descriptions on the FBI's Most Wanted list. "No can do, I'm afraid."

"It's really important." Prue nudged Piper, a not-so-subtle hint that she should get ready to freeze the guard where he stood. Then they could take the stairs to the third floor.

"I'm sorry," the man said, "but Mr. Jefferson left for his campaign headquarters half an hour ago."

"Where is that exactly?" Phoebe asked.

"This building is closed. The door's over there." The guard scowled and made a shooing motion.

"Never mind, Phoebe," Prue said in a strained voice. "I know where it is."

"Okay." Phoebe noticed Prue's set jaw and flexing fingers. She took her by the shoulders and turned her toward the exit. "We're going."

Phoebe whispered in Prue's ear as they stalked across the lobby. "Being unhelpful is not a crime punishable by telekinetic temper tantrum."

"I wasn't going to do anything," Prue whispered back. "There's no unwritten law against thinking about it."

Piper paused at the door and looked back to get in the last word with the guard. "Thanks for all your help. I'm sure the district attorney will be glad to know you're on the job protecting public buildings and public defenders from the public."

Phoebe yanked her through the door.

"I'm not sorry." Piper fumed as they headed across the parking lot.

The security guard's manner no longer concerned Phoebe. She patted her pocket to make sure the charm was still there and scanned the evening sky. The air was warm and still, but Athulak could be hovering anywhere, waiting to attack. She hoped Piper had read the potion directions correctly. Depending on cinnamon-scented chicken hearts for their safety pushed the limits of trust.

Piper stopped by her car and leaned on the door. "Do you need me for the campaign headquarters caper?"

Prue glanced at Phoebe.

Phoebe shrugged. She understood that Piper was

pressed to get everything ready for the bazaar tomorrow. The constant interruptions for rescues real and imagined had seriously interfered with her schedule. "I don't think so. I just have to touch Mr. Jefferson to find out what we need to know."

"What if you can't find him?" Piper asked.

Bazaar or no bazaar, Phoebe realized, Piper wouldn't shirk her duty to protect an innocent. However, direct contact with Noel Jefferson was absolutely essential. "No problem. We can probably find something that belongs to Mr. Jefferson at his campaign office."

Prue nodded. "And if not, we can ask Darryl to find him for us."

"Good idea!" Phoebe brightened. Having a contact within the police department came in handy, especially since Detective Darryl Morris knew they were witches.

"Okay, but call me if you run into trouble." Piper slipped behind the wheel, closed the door, and waved as she drove off.

Phoebe stared out the side window as Prue drove through the downtown nightlife districts as fast as traffic and traffic lights allowed. At eight o'clock, with daylight surrendering to the encroaching shadows of imminent darkness, all the restaurants and clubs were filling up. Couples sat at window tables, sipping drinks with gazes locked or strolled the sidewalks holding hands. Ignorance was bliss, Phoebe thought with unabashed envy.

She smiled, thinking of Rick and wondering if

he was as intelligent as he was handsome and if he was as nice as he seemed. If circumstances had been different last night and they had had a chance to talk, he might have asked her out to dinner tonight.

And she would have had to break the date to save Noel Jefferson and the world from some unknown but horrible fate.

The weight of responsibility was a big pain in the butt sometimes. Phoebe sighed.

"I know this is hard on you, Phoebe." Prue spoke without taking her eyes off the road.

"Yeah." Shifting her gaze frontward, Phoebe sighed again. "I know it's not easy for Piper with Leo being gone so much, but at least she's got someone who knows and understands that our lives are not entirely our own."

"What are you talking about?" Prue cast a quick, perplexed glance in Phoebe's direction.

"Men." Phoebe grinned. "Is there anything else?"

"There is tonight," Prue said. "We'll find the loves of our lives one of these days."

"I'm sure we will," Phoebe agreed. "If we ever find time to hunt for them."

Prue shot her a pointed look. "Unless Rick turns out to be a total jerk, your hunting days could be over."

"We'll probably have a great time for a while, but sooner or later the witch factor will ruin it. There will be questions I won't be able to answer honestly, broken dates I can't explain, and so on and so forth. Doomed from the start."

"Isn't that being a little too pessimistic?" Prue

asked without looking at Phoebe, her pensive gaze fastened on the road ahead.

"No, just being realistic." Phoebe sighed.

"Except that maybe none of that will matter when the *right* man comes along," Prue said.

Phoebe wanted to believe Prue, but she wasn't going to delude herself. For now she'd just take everything one step at a time. Rick hadn't even asked her out to dinner yet!

"There it is." Prue pointed at a strip mall on the right.

The Jefferson for Congress campaign headquarters occupied an office at the far end of the retail complex. Lights blazed inside and out, and a dozen people were visible through the large front windows. Phoebe fought off a surge of anxiety as Prue pulled into a parking space. She hadn't considered a scenario in which she had to brave a crowd to get to the main man.

"Ready?" Prue dropped her keys in her bag and opened the door.

"Yeah, but—" Phoebe hesitated. She didn't want to admit she was afraid of having her mind crash and burn from too much input, but she had to be honest. "Try to run point for me as much as you can, okay? The fewer people I touch, the better."

"Will do." Prue smiled, but her eyes couldn't hide her concern. "Let's go."

Phoebe braced herself as she followed Prue into the bustling office. Red-white-and-blue bunting adorned the back wall, lending a festive contrast to the line of gray metal filing cabinets underneath.

Posters featuring Jefferson's smiling face were plastered on the wall space that wasn't filled with rally schedules, membership forms for his political party, and other campaign paraphernalia. None of the people who were furiously sorting and stapling papers, manning the phone banks, or engaged in heated arguments seemed to notice them as they entered.

Phoebe wrapped her arms around herself to reduce the chance of rubbing elbows with the people sitting at a front table. They were all talking into telephones and scribbling on pledge cards.

"Jefferson's not in here," Prue said after a cursory scan of the room. "I'm going to ask the man at that desk over there."

"Where you lead, I will follow." Phoebe stuck close as Prue approached the desk. She didn't know a young woman had burst through the door behind her until it was too late to avoid contact.

"Hey, Mace!" The pretty young redhead in heels and a stylish hunter green suit pushed between Phoebe and Prue, waving a paper.

Phoebe staggered and clawed at Prue with grasping fingers as the vision hit.

. . . *scalding coffee pouring over her hand, white skin turning red and erupting with blisters* . . .

Phoebe's head began to pound, and her stomach churned as the impression faded. Breathless, she pointed Prue toward the redhead, who handed the man at the desk the paper, then moved toward a table set up for coffee. "Coffee," Phoebe rasped.

Prue eased Phoebe into a space between a pile of

cardboard boxes and the edge of the desk. "Don't move!"

"Don't worry." Phoebe concentrated on slowing her racing pulse and kept an eye on Prue, who intercepted the woman just as she reached the restaurant-style coffee machine and picked up a cup. The redhead pointed down a hall as they exchanged a few words. Prue casually placed another cup under the spigot.

"Jenny!"

The young woman jerked her head up and looked back at a man racing down the hall with a clipboard. "What's up, Charlie?"

Charlie ripped a sheet off the clipboard and handed it to her. "Channel Seven needs a Jefferson spokesperson for the late news. You're elected."

Phoebe stepped back as Jenny barreled past and out the door. She felt good in spite of her throbbing temples and shaky knees. Both the young woman and Mr. Jefferson would have missed a golden PR opportunity if Prue hadn't prevented the young woman from burning her hand.

"Phoebe!" Prue waved for Phoebe to join her in the hallway.

Checking both ways for frenzied campaign workers, Phoebe scurried past the desk. The man sitting behind it was shouting into the phone and didn't notice her. The lack of security was disturbing given that Mr. Jefferson was in dire danger from sources they hadn't discovered yet.

"We're in luck," Prue said. "Jefferson has an office at the end of this hall, and the candidate is in."

"Let's do it." Phoebe forced a smile and tried to muster some enthusiasm. However, any hope she had of getting a direct line to Jefferson's future through personal contact was dashed when she saw two large men sitting outside his door.

"This could be a problem," Phoebe whispered. The two men had stood up and snapped to alert attention when she and Prue had entered the hall.

"I know." Prue spoke softly through a fixed smile. "If I fling them out of the way, someone will call the cops, and it's too late to call Piper."

"So much for hindsight." Phoebe donned her brightest smile as she and Prue drew closer. She doubted the two men really considered two women a threat they couldn't handle. "Hey, guys! What's happening?"

"That's what I was about to ask you." The tall man on the left had a bushy mustache and was built like a linebacker. He clasped his hands in front of him and rocked back on his heels.

"We know you don't have an appointment." The man on the right was leaner with a steely gray stare that dispelled any illusion of weakness. He was all business all the time.

"You're right, we don't," Prue said. "But we really do need to see Mr. Jefferson on a matter of huge importance. It won't take more than a few minutes."

"Not a chance." Mr. Gray Eyes set his jaw with a stubborn determination that eerily resembled Prue when she dug in her heels. "Mr. Jefferson is in conference with his campaign manager, and he doesn't want to be disturbed. No arguments, no exceptions."

Phoebe waited to take her cues from Prue.

"I see." Prue sighed and sagged. "Well, you're just doing your jobs." She looked up suddenly, cocking her head and smiling with a coquettish twinkle in her eye. "Do you guard over Mr. Jefferson *all* the time?"

Tease, Phoebe thought, wondering what Prue was trying to accomplish. The lean, mean security machine was not her type.

"Twenty-four hours a day," the mustache said. "Where he goes, we go."

"No time off at all?" Prue asked.

Both men stared at her, immune to the bait.

Prue nudged Phoebe and extended her hand to the man on the right. "Well, it's been very nice meeting you." She nudged Phoebe again and shot her an exasperated glance. "Hasn't it?"

"Huh?" Slow on the uptake, Phoebe suddenly realized that Prue wanted her to connect with the guards. If they were always with Jefferson, then they would be right in the middle of anything bad that happened to their boss. "It sure has!"

Bracing herself, Phoebe grabbed the burly, mustached man by the hand. She fully expected to be bludgeoned by a vision of such incredible violence she would blow a mental fuse. She got absolutely nothing. The security guard did not have so much as a hangnail in his immediate future.

On the chance that the two men took alternate days off, Phoebe turned to the other guard and touched his arm. Again, nothing. "Nice coat."

Prue just stared at Phoebe a moment, stunned

because she was still standing and not stricken by a vision of Jefferson's death and destruction.

"Well, guess we'll be going." Phoebe shook Prue's arm. "We'll just make an appointment on our way out."

"Don't bother trying the window," the mustache said. "There isn't one."

"Right." Prue didn't need any urging to beat a fast retreat.

They did not stop to discuss the unexpected outcome of the encounters until they were back in the car.

"You didn't see anything?" Prue asked as she turned the ignition key.

"Nope." Phoebe threw up her hands in a gesture of helplessness. "The iron men are not in danger from anything worse than a pillow fight."

"So what does that mean?" Prue put the car in gear but applied the brakes instead of pulling out.

"I don't know." Phoebe shrugged, stymied. "Maybe they aren't with Jefferson at ground zero."

"I didn't get the feeling they were joking about being on duty twenty-four seven," Prue said.

"Neither did I," Phoebe agreed, her mind racing to come up with a plausible explanation. "The election is still weeks away. I suppose it's possible that whatever's going to happen doesn't happen soon."

Prue considered that a moment. "Possibly. Athulak granted your wish and the little girl's wish right away. It's been over two days since Tremaine made his."

"A wish with cataclysmic consequences would

probably take longer to develop and implement."
As she spoke, Phoebe had the unsettling feeling
they were still missing a piece of the puzzle. She
just couldn't figure out what. "I am pretty sure
there's nothing to worry about tonight. So, since we
have to rise and shine early tomorrow to help Piper,
we might as well go home and get some sleep."

Prue frowned. "How early?"

"Before the birds if you want coffee and time to
read the morning paper." Phoebe grinned as Prue
rolled her eyes and drove toward the street.

Leaning back, Phoebe closed her eyes and quietly
slipped back into the grip of despair. The dull ache in
her head wouldn't let her forget that Noel Jefferson
wasn't the only target of Athulak's lethal wrath.

She pulled Piper's protection charm out of her
pocket and held it in a tight fist, remembering the severed flagpole. She might not be sure about Noel
Jefferson's ultimate fate, but one thing was quite clear.

Athulak hated witches.

CHAPTER
11

Piper removed a batch of blueberry muffins from the oven and set them on the stove to cool. It was going to be a long day and she wanted to make sure both her sisters were fueled and ready to go the distance. The participation of local and national celebrities at the charity bazaar meant the event would be swarming with reporters. One picture of Brad Pitt stopping by her booth in the newspapers and P3 would leap into prominence as one of the hottest clubs in the state.

She paused to stare wistfully into space, imagining herself sitting beside Brad in a front-page photo, wondering if his appearance today was confirmed or just a rumor. Three weeks ago Leo had crossed-his-heart promised her that he would be at the bazaar, and she hadn't seen or heard from him since.

"I can't take Brad being a no-show, too!" Piper yanked the refrigerator door open to siphon off her frustration. If the big bosses on high thought she couldn't handle being apart from Leo, he would be yanked from her life for good.

Phoebe ambled in, yawning and rubbing her eyes as Piper set a bowl of sliced fresh fruit on the table.

"Morning!" Piper singsonged with a bright smile, hiding her dismay because Phoebe was still in her nightshirt and fuzzy slippers. She hadn't even combed her hair, which was flat against her head on one side and tangled on the other. Piper didn't want to jump-start the day with an argument, but she couldn't help wondering what Phoebe had been doing for the thirty minutes since her alarm had gone off.

Phoebe grunted and yawned.

"Coffee's brewing and there's fresh muffins," Piper said.

Nodding, Phoebe stared at the coffee maker as though she could will the machine to drip faster. After a few seconds, she got a mug from the cupboard and pulled the half-full pot out from under the drip basket. Two or three drops of hot liquid sizzled on the burner before the automatic shutoff kicked in.

"That's still a little strong." Piper grimaced and gingerly took the hot muffins out of the tins and put them on a plate.

"Good." Shoving the pot back into the machine, Phoebe grabbed the milk from the fridge, snatched the morning newspaper off the counter, and sat down at the table.

Somebody was cranky this morning, Piper thought, annoyed. She set the muffins on the table, next to the fruit.

Phoebe was too engrossed in the newspaper to notice. Her coffee sat untouched as she ran her finger down the page, then flipped the paper open and continued her intense search while nibbling her lower lip.

What was Phoebe's problem this morning? Piper wondered, blowing a wisp of hair off her forehead. According to her and Prue's report last night, Phoebe had gotten off easy with one minor vision and two blanks.

"Is Prue up yet?" Piper stood with her arms folded staring at Phoebe, who remained oblivious to everything but the morning news. "Did I tell you I'm going to live with Leo on the higher plane?"

"Uh-huh." Picking up her mug, Phoebe sipped and turned another page.

"I can't believe I'm up and it's still dark outside." Fresh from the shower, Prue waltzed in. Her black hair gleamed from vigorous brushing. A smoky blue scoop-neck top with three-quarter sleeves and tailored black pants emphasized the dazzle in her blue eyes. Prue looked like the after to Phoebe's before.

"Coffee's ready." Piper poured two cups and handed one to Prue. "Refill, Phoebe?"

"Sure." Phoebe set down her mug, tossed the front section of the paper on the floor, and moved on to the metro section.

Piper moved to the table, refilled the mug, then stood with her hand on one hip hitched to the side in a classic annoyed waitress pose. "Okay. What's the matter?"

Prue walked over and stared at Phoebe, too.

Seconds passed before Phoebe realized she was the focus of their intense scrutiny. She looked up slowly, her expression questioning. "Uh—problem?"

"You tell us." Piper left to put the coffeepot back on the warmer, then dropped into a chair beside Prue.

"We're listening," Prue said.

"Right." Piper nodded emphatically. "How come you aren't dressed? I had everything planned so we'd have plenty of time to enjoy breakfast before we have to leave for the park. So what gives?"

"I, uh, can't go." Phoebe's lip trembled, and she inhaled sharply on the verge of bursting into tears. "Too many people."

Piper's pique disintegrated in an emotional collision with sympathy for her sister and self-reproach. She had been so wrapped up with her own anxieties and excitement about the bazaar, she had dismissed the difficulties Phoebe was having with the extra visions. Worse, she realized. The additional strain had apparently taken a bigger toll than Phoebe had let on.

"How bad is it?" Piper's voice cracked and she cleared her throat.

"Pretty bad." Phoebe's hands shook when she picked up her mug.

"You seemed okay last night," Prue said.

"Yes and no." Taking a long swallow of coffee, Phoebe paused to massage her forehead.

Piper and Prue both waited patiently until she was ready to continue.

"The other day when the cashier cut her finger, the vision was like"—Phoebe paused, searching for the right words—"a whisper, but the physical effects are getting progressively more painful. And exhausting. The coffee burn Jenny didn't have because we stopped it was serious, but the effect the vision had on me was three times worse than it should have been. Understand?"

Prue nodded and gripped Phoebe's arm.

"Yeah." Ashamed, Piper averted her gaze and saw the newspaper on the floor. She picked it up, folded it, and set it on the table. "What were you looking for, Phoebe?" she asked gently.

Phoebe hung her head and sighed. "An article about Noel Jefferson's untimely demise."

"What?" Prue sat back, stricken. "But I thought—"

Phoebe held up a hand. "I didn't get anything from the two tough guys guarding the door. But after I went to bed, I kept thinking, what if they *aren't* right there with him when Athulak's catastrophe hits?"

"But they said—"

Phoebe interrupted Prue again. "I know. Twenty-four seven, but they are not with him *every* minute of every day and night. They were *outside* Jefferson's office last night, and he was inside—out of sight."

Prue's face went white. "You don't think Athulak paid him a visit, do you?"

Phoebe shook her head. "The disasters Athulak causes always relate to the actual wish, like the stampeding pony. He doesn't do his own dirty work."

"He certainly tried hard enough in the parking lot yesterday." Prue made a slashing motion across her throat.

Phoebe nodded. "But I'm guessing that he just hates witches. Wouldn't you want revenge if someone trapped you in a rock for three thousand years?"

"I might." Prue reached for a muffin and paused. "Should we call Darryl to see if Jefferson is all right?"

"No." Phoebe wiped a tear from the corner of her eye. "There's nothing in the paper, and I watched the news on TV when I got up."

Piper sensed Phoebe's misery and her dilemma. Because the visions had become so painful, she was questioning her motives for not trying harder to connect with Jefferson.

"You don't have anything to apologize for, Phoebe," Piper said. "You wouldn't have come home if you honestly thought something was going to happen to Jefferson last night."

"Yeah?" Phoebe tossed her head back with a short, derisive laugh. "If I really believed that, I would have gotten some sleep." She took several deep breaths to bring herself back from the brink of hysteria. "The thing is, what good is having my

power if I'm so intimidated by headaches and nausea that keep getting worse that I won't use it."

Prue sat bolt upright. "Ohmigod! That's it!"

"What?" Startled, Piper almost choked on her
coffee.

"Athulak's hidden agenda." Excited, Prue leaned
forward. "Yesterday we couldn't figure out his motive
for granting Phoebe's wish because her increased sensitivity was *preventing* disaster, not creating chaos."

"I'm with you so far," Piper said, "but I don't
understand where you're going."

"You talk, I'll eat." Phoebe pulled the muffin
plate toward her and leaned over to get a fork from
the drawer.

"Okay. This is going to sound complicated, but
it's not," Prue explained. "Not when you put it all
together in context."

Piper made a hurry-up motion and unwrapped a
muffin.

Prue took a sip of coffee and cleared her throat.
"We have to start with Tremaine's wish, which had
two elements. First, it freed Athulak from the stone.
Second, when the wish is fulfilled it will have cataclysmic repercussions."

"Agreed." Piper pointed to the silverware drawer.

Phoebe pulled out two more forks. She handed
one to Piper and placed the other by Prue.

"Now, since Tremaine's wish is taking longer to
grant than the others—the pony and Phoebe's
power," Prue clarified, "it could be that the first wish
is a lot more important to Athulak than just bumping
off a few humans or making them miserable."

"Important how?" Phoebe frowned. She looked as confused as Piper felt.

"Maybe it's do or die for Athulak." Prue paused, weighing her words. "What if his ultimate destiny depends on the first wish?"

"If something goes wrong and Tremaine's wish isn't granted, Athulak is history?" Phoebe asked for clarification.

"I love the theory," Piper said, "but it's really just a good guess, isn't it?"

"Not really." Prue stood up and went to the counter to get the coffeepot.

"It definitely falls into the category of wishful thinking for me, but I'm more than willing to be convinced." Phoebe jabbed an orange slice with her fork.

Prue topped off everyone's cup with coffee as she explained. "The key to the whole scenario is Noel Jefferson, the target of Tremaine's wish." Prue sat down and set the pot aside. "If Phoebe connects with Jefferson, we'll *know* how Tremaine's wish will be fulfilled."

"And if we know, we might be able to stop whatever happens from happening," Piper added.

Phoebe stopped chewing to stare at her sisters. "Right, but how did Athulak figure that out?"

As the clues sank in, Piper suddenly found that all the pieces did fall neatly into place. Athulak had seen Prue use her powers in Tremaine's library and had followed her to the park. He had been imprisoned by a witch and was worried that a modern witch might interfere with his plans.

"Athulak was at the park when Phoebe sounded the alert about the runaway pony *before* it bolted." Piper sat back, stunned. "We even talked about meeting Noel Jefferson at the charity bazaar today."

"That's how I see it," Prue said. "When Athulak discovered that Phoebe could see the future, he realized she might see the catastrophe in *Jefferson's* future."

"So when Phoebe made her wish," Piper said, "Athulak enhanced her power to render her powerless."

"That is so disgustingly diabolical," Phoebe fumed.

"That's why they call them demons," Piper said.

Prue smiled at Phoebe. "But there was one crucial factor he didn't take into account: your devotion to doing the right thing even though it might hurt you."

Phoebe, however, was not easily appeased. "I appreciate that, Prue, but I didn't follow through. We didn't get close enough to Noel Jefferson for me to have a vision."

"But you intended to," Prue reminded Phoebe. "Where were we going when he attacked us?"

Phoebe blinked. "To see Noel Jefferson."

"Yep." Prue picked up her muffin and peeled off the paper cup. "I rest my case."

"I'll buy the theory, but I still haven't completed the mission." Phoebe set her fork down, her expression pained. "We have no idea how Athulak plans to get Noel Jefferson out of the election."

"It's not too late to find out," Piper said. "Jefferson

is still scheduled to give a speech at the bazaar this morning. Around eleven, I think."

"I'll go get dressed." Phoebe rushed out of the room.

"Well, I guess we'd better not waste any time." Piper carried the muffin plate and the fruit bowl to the counter.

"We're going to need at least another hour." Prue picked up the coffeepot and put it back in the machine. "I don't know about you, but I'll feel a lot better having a *fresh* protection charm on me today."

Piper handed Prue a roll of cellophane wrap. "You clean up. I'll cook."

Piper's nerves were on edge as she gathered the ingredients and unfolded the directions for the protection potion. The wind spirit apparently had the ability to manipulate his form into a deadly molecular blade. He could also wield it with enough force to slice through a steel pole. Three flesh-and-bone necks would be a snap by comparison. He had tried to kill once to keep Phoebe from touching Noel Jefferson. It would be foolish to think he wouldn't try again.

The charms were their only defense. Maybe, Piper thought as she retrieved a plastic container of raw chicken hearts from the fridge. There was another, ominous possibility no one had considered. Since Phoebe had been locked in the rest room when Jefferson had left the municipal building, Athulak may have simply followed him. He would have known Prue and Phoebe couldn't get past the security men at his campaign headquarters and may have even tailed them home to be sure.

Piper stared at the falcon feathers sealed in a zippered plastic bag with a sinking sensation in the pit of her stomach. The spell she had gotten from *The Book of Shadows* had been written to repel tornadoes and hurricanes. She had adjusted it to include a sentient evil that had taken form as air.

She had absolutely no proof that the protection charms worked.

CHAPTER
12

Even though the Celebrity Charity Bazaar did not open officially until nine, the grounds were bustling with activity when Prue pulled into the parking lot at eight.

"Do we know where your booth is?" Prue asked Piper as the sisters got out of the car. While some vendors had come with their own setups, complete with generators, Piper had rented a booth with access to electricity from the organizers. Most of those were located near the pavilions on the far side of the picnic area.

"Not exactly." Piper looked up from a diagram of the booth layout the organizers had sent her and held her hand above her eyes to survey the park. She glanced at the diagram again, then pointed to a pavilion shaded by tall palms and hardwoods to their left. "I think we're over there."

Shouldering her camera bag, Prue locked the car doors. Although another bag of extra gear was stuffed under the seat, she didn't want to take any chances.

Phoebe leaned against the hood with her arms folded close to her chest, a stance that drove home just how loath she was to touch anyone. Above all, Prue thought, renewing the vow she and Piper had made when Phoebe had left the kitchen to change, Phoebe had to be protected from physical contact with anyone except Noel Jefferson. Saving the future congressman and the world was imperative.

"I hope Jimmy and the gang arrived on time to take our deliveries." Piper exhaled nervously.

"I wonder if Rick showed up," Prue said.

"Don't know, but I'm off to find out. I'll see you as soon as I know everything is under control." Gripping the strap of her shoulder bag, Piper left to find her booth.

Prue glanced at Phoebe, but her teasing reference to Rick had gone unheard. Her sister's somber gaze was trained on the silent amusement park located at the northern end of the picnic grounds. Dominated by the towering Ferris wheel, a huge, ornate carousel, and a roller coaster that was tame by contemporary standards, the Gold Coast Amusement Park had sprawled across the landscape like a slow-growing amoeba since it had first opened decades before. However, over the past several months there had been talk of closing the old attraction down.

"Penny for your thoughts," Prue said.

Phoebe's gaze darted to Prue, then back to the amusement park. "I've never been here when Gold Coast was closed. It's kind of spooky, as if it died when the lights and the rides were turned off and the screams and the circus music faded into"—she paused, her eyes misting—"echoes of more innocent, happier times, maybe. When we were kids."

"That's awfully profound for so early in the day." Prue tried to offset Phoebe's melancholy, but she knew that Phoebe would find a way to overcome this personal crisis, too. A code of no surrender had been bred into the Halliwell bloodline for centuries.

"Okay." Straightening up, Phoebe flashed Prue a smile. "I've indulged in all the doom and gloom I can stand for one day. Let's take care of business so we can have some fun."

"I'm ready." Prue glanced in the direction Piper had gone. "Do you want to help Piper or go with me to check out the stage where Tremaine and Jefferson will be speaking?"

Phoebe's internal struggle was evident on her face.

"I'll understand if you'd rather hang out with Rick," Prue added.

The light that shone from Phoebe's eyes at the mention of Rick faded almost immediately. "Work first. Play later."

"Let's go then." Prue led the way toward a large wooden pavilion. A large blue-and-white canvas canopy had been erected just beyond it. Inside the pavilion, crews were securing risers that formed a stage, setting up folding chairs for the audience, and running cables for the sound system. Singing groups from local schools, aspiring bands, and the celebrities would share the program with the politicians.

Phoebe stuck close to Prue's side as they made their way up a wide jogging path. Except for people carting in supplies and products, the path was clear of traffic, and Phoebe began to relax. Most of the vendors were off to the side, furiously working on their booths.

"Oh, look at those rag dolls!" Phoebe exclaimed. The woman unpacking the antique-style cloth dolls outfitted in calico dresses and off-white eyelet pinafores with matching caps held one out for Phoebe's inspection. Phoebe shook her head. "Maybe later."

"What do you want with a rag doll?" Prue asked, delighted that Phoebe was taking an interest in something besides their unpleasant mission.

"They're adorable!" Phoebe shrugged with a sheepish smile. "She'd look darling on my bed."

A darling reminder of bygone days and more innocent times, Prue noted with a smile. As she looked around, she realized that the whole bazaar had been designed to promote a sense of community and goodwill.

The wares displayed in the booths ranged from handcrafted jewelry and wooden toys, foreign food and hot dogs, to hot tubs and exercise equipment. Other booths were devoted to organizations: citizen activist and political groups, education and health care programs, businesses like P3, and sponsors of team sports and other family recreational activities. Prue was impressed with the diversity, ingenuity, and enthusiasm of the participants. She wondered if the other vendors had driven their families crazy making preparations for the big event. Piper had obviously known what she was doing when she had signed on, though. Judging from the displays, everyone was expecting a huge crowd.

"I smell coffee." Phoebe paused to inhale the enticing aroma wafting from the tent. "I could use another cup or two."

"Ditto that," Prue said as she calculated her next move.

Two sides under the canopy were open but roped off to discourage entry. A wall of blue-and-white striped canvas closed off the rearside. The side facing the pavilion was partially roped off to form an entrance. Tables and chairs were arranged in the center under the canopy. Two women were filling trays with Danish and doughnuts on tables along the back wall. The tables also contained two large, banquet-style coffee machines, creamer, sugar, and several varieties of tea, a water cooler, and tubs of iced soft drinks. A sign over the entrance read, Press and Official Guests Only.

"I don't suppose we qualify as official guests, huh?" Phoebe frowned, annoyed.

"No, but we might qualify as official press." Prue fished her 415 press pass out of her leather shoulder bag and handed the camera bag to Phoebe. "You just got hired to assist."

"You are so bad." Phoebe grinned.

"I know." Prue cut her laugh short as she walked toward the tent with the air of someone who knew exactly who she was and where she was going.

An attractive young woman seated at a small table by the entrance blinked as Prue walked in without giving her a glance. "Wait a minute! Miss!"

Prue stopped, motioned Phoebe to continue on, then turned to the woman with a puzzled frown. "Yes?"

"Uh—this tent isn't open to the public." The woman, Louise according to her nametag, seemed genuinely apologetic when she pointed up toward the sign. "Press and guests only, I'm afraid."

Prue stepped up to the table and held out her press pass. "Prue Halliwell, photographer from 415." She glanced at Phoebe. "And my assistant."

Louise squinted at the pass. "Oh, cool!" She smiled. "Help yourself to whatever and make yourself comfortable."

"Thanks," Prue said, smiling back. "My editor told me to capture the local flavor of the bazaar. Would you mind if I took a shot of you for the magazine?"

"Me?" Flustered, Louise smoothed her short dark hair. "Uh—no. I mean, that would be great."

"Excellent!" Prue started to leave, then stepped back. "Do you know when Mr. Jefferson is speaking? I left my schedule in the car."

"Eleven o'clock. I just spoke to him, and he'll be here about a quarter of." Louise held up her cell phone as proof and leaned over to speak confidentially. "I talked to Whoopi this morning, too. She's going to be late."

"Well, at least she's coming. Thanks again. I'll be back in a few minutes." Confident that she and Phoebe would have access to the tent all day, Prue got herself a coffee and joined Phoebe at a table in the back corner.

"Are we cool?" Phoebe cast a doubtful glance at Louise.

"Totally." Prue removed her camera from the bag and set it on the table. "If anyone asks, just mention my name and the magazine and say you're my assistant. Louise over there will back you up."

"I can do that." Phoebe tensed when two women and a man with clipboards and briefcases seated themselves at the next table over. However, they were intent on their own business and paid no attention to Phoebe and Prue.

"So what's the plan?" Phoebe lowered her voice. "Do we have a plan?"

"We do now." Prue leaned toward her. "But first the good news. Louise just spoke to Jefferson. No mishaps in the middle of the night."

Phoebe's hand flew to her chest in a gesture of relief. "Thank goodness. What do we do next?"

"You're going to sit right here and wait while I go check in with Piper," Prue said. "It might get a little crowded, but better to hobnob with the celebs than take a chance in the crowds out there."

Phoebe nodded, smiling. "We've had worse plans. Bruce Willis isn't on the guest list, is he?"

"Bruce Willis?" Prue eyed Phoebe askance.

"Since when is Bruce Willis at the top of your famous-movie-stars-I'd-like-to-meet list?"

"He's sexy and cute," Phoebe said, "for an old guy. Like Mel Gibson and Harrison Ford."

"It's your fantasy." Prue stood and picked up the camera. "I think I'd better wander around and play photographer for appearances' sake. I don't want Louise to get suspicious and throw us out."

"Not with five dozen doughnuts to choose from," Phoebe quipped.

"Jefferson won't be here for a couple more hours, but I'll be back before then. With luck you can make contact right here in the tent before he delivers his speech." Prue noticed a subtle shift in Phoebe's cheerful demeanor. "Are you sure you'll be okay waiting here alone?"

"Are you kidding?" Perking up again, Phoebe spread her arms to encompass the VIP domain. "I've got plenty of coffee and an in with the in crowd. What more could I ask?"

Priming the camera, Prue left to snap a few shots and seal the deal with Louise.

"You guys are doing great!" Piper pulled off the ponytail holder and shook out her hair. For the first time in a week, she felt as though she had made a sound decision to invest her limited PR money in the booth.

Jimmy, Rick, and two of Jimmy's friends had finished getting the tables, stools and chairs, the refrigerator, and other equipment in place with amazing speed and efficiency. They even had the electrical cables ready for Hard Crackers when the band arrived to set up right after noon. Until then Jimmy's taped collection of easy rock would set the right mood.

Sandy and Monica, Piper's two waitresses for the event, bopped to the sounds of an old Cars song as they topped off the tables with red- and white-checkered cloths and pots of red geraniums. Napkin holders doubled as paperweights to keep stacks of P3 flyers from drifting away on a light breeze.

The Celebrity Charity Bazaar promised to be a huge success, as long as Athulak didn't sweep down from the sky bent on revenge. Piper touched the charm in her pocket and rubbed a kink in her neck. Her sudden decapitation would probably get Leo's attention, wherever he was, but she seriously doubted his healing powers could put her back together again.

"Wow! This looks fantastic!" Prue came up from behind Piper, folded her arms and nodded as she surveyed the nearly completed booth.

Piper beamed in spite of her distressing thoughts. "You don't think it's too much? I mean, we don't have flowers on the tables at P3."

"No, it's perfect. I love what you did with the photos." Prue walked over to the easel Piper had set to the left of the booth. The pictures of P3 in action were tacked to a bulletin board resting on the wooden stand. "These came out pretty well, didn't they?"

"Yes, thank you." Piper caught herself holding her neck and jammed her hands in her pockets. "Any word on the Mr. Jefferson situation?"

"I found out that he's definitely alive and well this morning. He's expected to arrive for his speech about a quarter to eleven."

Piper pulled a folded schedule from her pocket. "Tremaine is speaking right after him at eleven forty-five."

Prue frowned. "I wonder if that works into Athulak's plan. We'll know if Phoebe can get a read on Jefferson before he speaks." Prue took a quick look around for curious ears. "I know we can't use our you-know-what in this crowd, but you should probably be there just in case."

"Moral support if nothing else." Piper knew they'd use their powers if they had to, but only as a last resort. She glanced back toward the stage pavilion. "Where is Phoebe?"

"In the VIP tent, hoping to run into Bruce Willis." Prue set her camera on the counter that ran the length of the booth, then slid onto a stool. She jumped when Rick popped up on the far side holding a wrench.

"Phoebe knows Bruce Willis?" Rick's brow furrowed under a shock of unruly blondish hair.

"That's news to me, too." Piper perched on the stool beside her. "Although I'm glad you brought your camera. When Brad Pitt stops by, there probably won't be a reporter in sight."

Rick's mouth fell open. "You know Brad Pitt?"

"We're just friends." Piper burst out laughing. "Not."

"Don't worry, Rick," Prue said. "I happen to know Phoebe likes tall guys with sandy blond hair. Bruce is short and practically bald."

Rick's obvious interest in Phoebe seemed to have short-circuited his sense of humor, Piper realized. He obviously didn't get the joke.

"Phoebe doesn't know any movie stars," Piper added.

Phoebe stared at the gray-haired man sitting across the table from her, fascinated. He wasn't Bruce Willis, but she had seen him in dozens of movies and television cop shows over the years. His name, however, completely escaped her.

"The best part was when he bent over and split the back seam of his pants," the old actor chuckled. "He made them destroy the film."

"Had to protect the old he-man image, huh?" Phoebe smiled.

"He-man with a glass jaw." The old actor looked up, a twinkle in his eye. "But you didn't hear that from me."

"I'm really good at keeping secrets," Phoebe said.

"Well, I'm still getting bit parts here and there. Nobody's seen *him* on the big screen in ten years. Not on the little screen, either." The man's glee was infectious and Phoebe laughed.

After Prue had left her, she had spent an hour reading the gothic paperback novel she had stuck in her bag. She had passed the next thirty minutes gawking at the local television news personalities and numerous character actors she recognized. They drifted in and out of the tent, taking breaks from mingling with the crowd, or used it as a green-room before speaking or performing to encourage donations to the charity fund. Most of the minor celebrities had ignored her. A few had smiled or nodded or said hello in passing, which was just as well because she didn't know any of their names, either.

Then her charming, elderly companion had wandered over with a doughnut in one hand, a cup of coffee in the other, and asked if he could sit down. She could hardly refuse since the chair at her table was the only vacant seat under the tent. She had spent the last half hour listening to his stories about working on various sets.

There was just one problem. He had touched her hand when he had reached for a napkin.

The vision was the first she had had all day and the effects weren't as bad as they might have been. Through the sheer force of will, she had sat still through the vicious hammering in her head and the rush of nausea without collapsing, but that wasn't the problem. How, Phoebe wondered, was she supposed to tell this sweet, cantankerous old guy his false teeth were going to fall out onstage?

"There's Noel now." A woman at the next table gathered her papers and stuffed them into a briefcase.

Phoebe straightened to look past the old man at the entrance to the tent. Tall and blond with a boyish grin, Jefferson entered surrounded by a large entourage. Phoebe recognized Jenny the redhead, Charlie with the clipboard, the mustache, and his lean, mean partner from their visit to Jefferson's campaign headquarters last night. There were at least a dozen other men and women in the group, some of whom were reporters.

There was no sign of Piper and Prue.

"Who's that?" The old man shifted in his chair to look at the commotion.

"Noel Jefferson," Phoebe said. "He's running for Congress."

When the mass of people shifted, Phoebe realized Jefferson had his hand on the back of a pretty woman with blond hair wearing a wide-brimmed straw hat. The woman was holding the hand of a freckle-faced boy who looked about eight.

Not married but appears to be very involved, Phoebe thought with a flash of regret for Prue. Their picnic discussion about the candidate as a romantic possibility for Prue had been in jest. Still, even a casual flirtation for fun was out of the question if the guy had his girlfriend along.

Phoebe checked her watch and stood up. Jefferson was on in five minutes.

"Darn politicians get more publicity than actors these days." The old actor snorted and shook his head as he turned back around. "Don't tell me you're leaving? I was just getting warmed up!"

"Yeah. I'd love to stay and listen, but I really have to go." Resolved, Phoebe bent over and whispered in his ear. There was no way she could stand by and let him embarrass himself in front of all these people. "This is a little awkward, but I think you should check your dentures before you give your talk. Don't be mad."

He reached up and squeezed her arm. "I'm not. Thank you."

"If I can, I'll be watching." Phoebe quickly moved to the food tables where the knots of people weren't so concentrated. She wasn't worried about Jefferson's bodyguards trying to stop her today. The candidate was shaking every hand within reach, hoping to get votes. However, if she had a vision triggered by someone else before she reached him, the opportunity would be lost. She studied the room and chose a course that would work as long as nobody shifted position.

Holding her arms close to her body, Phoebe wove her way around tables without incident. She stopped a few feet from the crowd gathered around Jefferson to figure out where to go next.

"What's your stand on campaign finance reform," a newscaster asked.

Jefferson didn't try to evade a direct answer. "We have to keep soft money out of politics so our elected representatives at every level aren't in the pockets of the special interests. The government's first and only priority should be to the people who vote them into office."

Under different circumstances, Phoebe would have cheered.

The reporters and TV news teams were concentrated in front of Jefferson. The mustache and the mean guy stood slightly behind and to the sides of the candidate, his date, and the kid. Beyond the group, she saw Prue and Piper waving frantically.

A quick glance around made it clear that Piper

could not freeze the scene to help her out. Aside from the people in the crowded tent, swarms of people were streaming by. There were easily a hundred people sitting in the audience waiting to hear Jefferson's speech. Almost all of them were watching the impromptu press conference.

"I want a doughnut." The kid tugged on his mother's hand.

The woman leaned down and hushed him. "In a minute, Paul."

Catching Prue's eye, Phoebe raised her hand and pointed to indicate she was going to try to get close to Jefferson from the rear. Using the crowd as a shield would be safer. If she keeled over after shaking the candidate's hand, she'd attract too much attention. Touching his arm or shoulder was all the contact she needed, and nobody would notice if she collapsed on the back fringe of the gathering.

Prue and Piper exchanged a word, then Prue ducked under the ropes to improve her position.

Skirting the outer fringe, taking care not to touch anyone, Phoebe was halfway to her goal when the entire gathering seemed to shift as one entity. They all surged forward as the MC called Jefferson onto the stage.

Phoebe clenched her fists, not sure what to do.

Prue raised her hand and shot her a questioning glance.

Piper watched helplessly from outside the tent.

Knowing they might not have another chance if Jefferson eluded them this time, Phoebe moved behind Jefferson just as the guards began to close

ranks to protect his back. As the candidate started
to turn toward the stage, she lunged.

In the same split second, the kid yanked his hand
out of his mother's grasp, spun, and ran into
Phoebe.

Thrown backward by the boy's momentum,
Phoebe sprawled on the ground as she was swept
into the maelstrom of the vision.

. . . *clinging to a metal bar . . . the boy screaming in
terror . . . watching Noel Jefferson fall from the top of the
Ferris wheel . . .*

CHAPTER
13

Prue could not believe how fast things had gone so wrong.

"Paul!" the woman in the straw hat yelled as Phoebe collapsed on the floor.

Prue saw Noel Jefferson look back as she shoved through the jam of reporters.

"What happened?" Jefferson frowned.

"Nothing to worry about, sir." The large security guard urged the candidate to keep moving toward the stage.

The guard with the gray eyes turned as the boy's mom knelt beside him. Several reporters blocked the guard's view of Phoebe, and he quickly turned back to Jefferson.

"I didn't mean to." The boy sniffed back tears. "But you said I could have a doughnut!"

"It's all right, Paul." The woman reached out to touch Phoebe, who was curled up, clutching her stomach, her face contorted with pain.

Prue gripped the woman's shoulder, staying her hand. "Please, she's my sister."

"She seems to be in a lot of pain." The woman looked devastated as Prue eased around her and dropped down beside Phoebe. "I can't believe Paul hit her that hard."

Prue caught sight of Piper arguing with the young woman by the entrance. Pulling Phoebe's head into her lap, she smiled to reassure the boy's mother. "It wasn't his fault. She, uh—hasn't been well."

"Well, if you're sure." The woman seemed hesitant to go.

"I'm sure. She just needs some air. She'll be fine in a few minutes." Prue exhaled as the woman hustled the boy outside. He stopped crying when she promised to take him to the amusement park before they went home.

Since Paul had triggered Phoebe's vision, Prue watched to see where they went. The woman sat the boy on a chair close to the stage and stood beside him to listen to Jefferson's speech. One of the reporters immediately offered her his seat.

Satisfied that Paul was safe for the moment, Prue's gaze swung back to Piper as Phoebe moaned and started to come around. Piper raised her hand, intending to freeze the stubborn young woman at the entrance so she could enter.

"Piper!" Prue shook her head when Piper turned.

A smoldering anger simmered in Piper's brown

eyes, but the tension drained away when she saw Phoebe stir. Thumbing over her shoulder, she backed off.

"What happened?" an old man asked, startling Prue from behind. "Should I call 911?"

"No," Prue said a bit too sharply, aware of the many curious stares. She and Phoebe had already attracted too much attention for comfort.

Phoebe pushed herself into a sitting position and breathed in deeply. She smiled weakly at the old man and rasped, "I'll be fine. Really."

"She just needs to rest." Prue helped Phoebe to her feet and braced her with an arm around her waist. "I'll handle it."

Nodding, the concerned man stepped back as Prue walked Phoebe out of the tent.

Prue saw Piper pacing by a large tree a short distance behind the audience. As she and Phoebe walked past the seated crowd, she couldn't help but notice that Noel Jefferson's serene yet powerful voice had everyone enthralled. Listening to him talk about alternate energy sources and the need to preserve the country's dwindling wilderness areas for future generations just strengthened her resolve to do whatever was necessary to save him.

If they discovered the threat before it was too late, she thought with growing apprehension.

"How is she?" Piper's gaze mirrored Prue's worry.

"The boy." Phoebe's voice trembled with panic as she sank to the ground with Piper and Prue. "Where is he?"

"Listening to the speech," Prue said.

Relieved, Phoebe nodded and leaned back against the tree. "Good. Then we have time."

"Before what exactly?" Piper asked.

"And how serious is it?" Prue hated putting pressure on Phoebe in her weakened condition, but they were still no closer to stopping the fulfillment of Tremaine's wish than they were before. She did not want to think about having to choose between saving the boy or the candidate. "What happens to Paul, Phoebe?"

"I'm not sure he gets hurt, except for the trauma"—Phoebe shuddered—"when he sees Noel Jefferson fall from the top of the Ferris wheel."

Piper inhaled sharply and sat back on her heels.

Prue stared into Phoebe's tormented eyes. A bizarre twist of fate had given them the critical information they needed, but the boy's involvement was a shock. She thought back to Professor Rubin's explanation about Athulak, wondering if Paul also played a key role in the irreversible and catastrophic consequences that would result from Tremaine's wish. Would the effects of watching a man fall to his death pervert Paul's destiny, adding to the harm created when Tremaine was elected and not Noel Jefferson?

Prue quickly put those disquieting thoughts aside. There would be no chaotic chain of events if Jefferson survived, and that depended on them.

"I heard Paul's mom promise to take him to the amusement park," Prue said. "We'll just have to stop them from going."

"Works for me." Piper glanced across the park toward the P3 booth. "Jimmy and the girls can take care of things, and Rick decided to stick around in case the booth gets super busy."

"I wouldn't bet money that's the only reason." Prue smiled at Phoebe. "He's smitten with those big brown eyes."

"Yeah?" A smile flickered and died on Phoebe's face as she stood up. Still shaky, she steadied herself with a hand on the tree trunk. "If we're going to ambush Mr. Jefferson on his way to the amusement park, we should probably get behind the rocks."

"What rocks?" Piper asked, confused.

"I meant get in position," Phoebe clarified. "I'm not exactly moving at optimum efficiency right now."

"Good idea." Prue rose and dusted off the seat of her pants. "Let's move out."

Piper followed behind Prue and Phoebe as they slowly made their way to an empty picnic table a few hundred yards beyond the stage pavilion. She resisted the impulse to check the surrounding sky. If Athulak attacked, they wouldn't see him coming. The thought was chilling, and if the circumstances weren't so dire, she might have appreciated the irony. Of all the grotesque demons, vengeful warlocks, and other malevolent entities they had fought and vanquished, a being made of air might be their undoing.

"Any idea how long we have to wait?" Piper asked as she slid onto the picnic table bench.

Phoebe shook her head and swung her legs under the opposite side of the table.

"Probably not long," Prue said. She straddled the end of Phoebe's bench, facing the parking lot. "Paul will be pretty restless after sitting through Jefferson's speech."

"Too bad he's attached," Phoebe said with a pointed look at Prue. "Noel Jefferson, I mean. From what I saw, he and Paul's mom are like that." She held up crossed fingers.

"My only interest in Noel Jefferson is saving his life, the kid's life, and the world," Prue protested.

For starters anyway, Piper thought. She looked back toward the pavilion to check on Jefferson. His entourage was forming below the stage, and the audience was dispersing.

"Heads up," Piper warned.

"Any ideas how we're going to pull off this ambush?" Phoebe asked.

"I'm sure we'll think of something," Prue said. "I'm working on it."

Piper's gaze drifted toward the parking lot, her attention diverted by another group of TV news people and reporters, who were following Stephen Tremaine toward the pavilion. As they passed by, Tremaine glanced toward their table, hesitated, and did an abrupt right turn.

"Incoming," Piper whispered as the opposition candidate approached. The reporters hung back.

"Ms. Halliwell?" Tremaine zeroed in on Prue. Unlike Jefferson, who was wearing casual clothes suitable for an outside fair, Tremaine was dressed in a perfectly tailored suit and tie with expensive black shoes polished to a mirror shine.

"Mr. Tremaine." Prue smiled tightly. "What a surprise."

"I'm delighted to see you again as well." The candidate looked and sounded sincere. "Your editor sent me proofs of the photos you took the other day. I just wanted you to know how pleased I am with the results. Excellent work."

"Thank you." Prue smiled graciously but did not invite further conversation.

They didn't have time for a friendly chat, Piper realized when she saw Noel Jefferson's crowd coming toward them from the other direction.

Tremaine, however, was in no hurry to leave. He held his hand out to shake Piper's hand and bumped Phoebe's shoulder.

Phoebe's head snapped up and her eyes rolled back as she slumped over. Piper jumped onto the table and fell on her knees beside her stricken sister.

"What the—" Tremaine recoiled as Prue threw a protective arm over Phoebe's back. "Should we call an ambulance?"

"No, it's just the heat. Nothing to worry about," Prue explained hastily. "But it might be better if you leave."

Tremaine hesitated, then backed off and waved his people to follow.

Piper cradled Phoebe's head, realizing their problems had suddenly become dangerously more complicated. She watched helplessly as Noel Jefferson and company passed by on their way to the amusement park and a deadly ride on the Ferris wheel.

Beside her, Phoebe writhed in pain.

*   *   *

The mental images assaulted Phoebe with a force
as great as the annihilation they foretold. A silent
scream reverberated through her head as she saw
the beautiful city of San Francisco fast forward into
ruin and decay. Lighted windows on downtown
buildings went dark and shattered, raining slivers
of glass on deserted, torn-up streets. Green leaves
withered and fell off trees that smoked and disintegrated into char. Emaciated people stumbled
through alleys, deathly quiet and too weak to run.

She watched in horror as the image of the city
receded, giving her a panoramic view. Blanketed in
a thick gray haze one second, San Francisco van-
ished in thunder and a blinding light the next. Then
the image cut to black.

Tears streamed from Phoebe's eyes as she
emerged from the depths of future Armageddon.

"Come on, come on . . ."

Latching onto Prue's frantic voice, Phoebe forced
herself back to reality. The nausea had become a
burning knot, as though her stomach was being
eaten away by flaming bile. Sharp pains shot
through her head, making it difficult to focus.

"Phoebe." Piper gently shook her arm. "What
did you see? What happens to Tremaine?"

Pulse racing and barely able to breathe, Phoebe
dug her fingers into Piper's thigh and raised her
head. "He burns with everyone else," she whispered hoarsely. "Nuclear holocaust."

"How?" Prue gasped.

"Irrelevant." Phoebe glared at her sisters, draw-
ing strength from the Power of Three that bound

them together. "You're going to stop it by making sure Noel Jefferson lives to get elected."

Prue and Piper both looked toward the parking lot, then back at Phoebe, their eyes brimming with worry and indecision.

"Go!" Phoebe barked.

"Okay." Prue ran her hand over Phoebe's hair as she stood up. "We're going."

Laying her head back down, Phoebe watched her sisters run after the doomed candidate. Tears pooled on the rough wooden surface under her cheek and a shuddering sigh rumbled through her chest. There was nothing more she could do. The fate of the world rested on Prue's and Piper's shoulders now.

"How can one man cause a nuclear holocaust?" Piper asked as she and Prue came to a breathless stop by the Tilt-a-Whirl.

"Has Phoebe ever been wrong?" Hands on her knees, Prue kept an eye on Jefferson and calmed her ragged breathing. The cameramen, reporters, campaign workers, and Paul's mom moved off to the side as he stepped into the Ferris wheel line with the boy.

"No, she hasn't." As Piper pulled a ponytail holder out of her pocket, the leather protection charm popped out and fell on the ground. She dropped into a squat to pick it up.

In the same instant, Prue heard a high-pitched whine. The sound intensified as the temperature of the air around her face plunged to freezing.

Athulak! With no time to shout an alarm, Prue watched as her sister's fingers seemed to reach for the charm in excruciating slow motion. In her mind, she saw Piper's head roll, separated from her neck with a swift stroke of the wind spirit's molecular sword.

She blinked when the whine became a higher-pitched, keening cry of outrage and sensed that the invisible entity had suddenly veered off.

Piper stood up and slipped the charm back into her pocket, then pulled her hair back and secured it with the holder. Her eyes narrowed with bewilderment when she noticed Prue staring. "What?"

"The protection charm works." Prue straightened with a tight smile.

Piper looked up sharply to scan the sky, her hand darting to her neck. "You're sure?"

"Field tested and approved." Prue noted Piper's gasp as the significance of her words sank in, but they didn't have time to celebrate her narrow escape. Noel Jefferson and Paul were next up to get on the Ferris wheel. "Let's move. Somehow we have to talk Mr. Jefferson out of going on that ride."

Piper nodded and fell into a brisk walk beside Prue as the ride operator brought the next empty bucket to a stop over the loading platform. Jefferson let the boy get in first, paused to buckle his seat belt, then stepped inside and sat down.

Prue quickened her pace, having no idea what to say. Nothing convincing came to mind. They'd sound like deranged lunatics if they told him the truth.

The operator locked the safety bar in place and Prue broke into a run. "Wait!"

What to say ceased to be a problem when the bodyguards spun toward the sound of Prue's voice. They recognized her instantly. It didn't require much imagination to figure out what was going through their minds as they positioned themselves to the block the advance of two frantic, running women. Whether they thought she and Piper were overly zealous fans or a potential threat, the two men had no intention of letting them near their man.

Prue's heart fluttered when the operator started the wheel. Jefferson's bucket rose and lurched to a stop as the next bucket moved into place. It was the last empty bucket on the giant wheel.

"So much for talking." Piper said as they stopped and faced off the guards. "I'd say this qualifies as an emergency, wouldn't you?"

"Major emergency," Prue said. "Permission granted."

Piper froze the guards, the people in the immediate vicinity, and the wheel. Risky, Prue thought as they dashed past the other people waiting in line and the scowling men to jump into the bucket, but necessary.

"Buckle up," Piper said as she waved her hand to set real time back in motion.

The operator blinked, shrugged, and locked down the safety bar without giving their sudden appearance a second thought. Prue realized he went through the repetitive motions of his job with little or no change in routine, but she didn't breathe easily until he sat down on a metal stool and depressed the lever to start the ride.

Jefferson's two guards did not take her and Piper's disappearance quite so casually, Prue noted with satisfaction. They both jerked and looked from side to side, completely thrown off balance, with their grim confidence broken. When the mustached man looked over his shoulder and saw her, Prue smiled and waved.

"Stop that thing!" The guard stormed up to the operator. "Now!"

The operator rolled his eyes and shooed him away. "Scram, buddy!"

Riding the wheel upward under Jefferson's bucket, Prue stared back at the befuddled guards. Then, after the bucket rounded the top of the circle, she focused solely on Jefferson, whose bucket seat was below them on the downward side.

Neither she nor Piper spoke.

Gripping the safety bar, Piper stared down, too. Every muscle in her slim body was steeled, waiting for that critical split second when their powers could mean the difference between success and failure.

The wheel went around and around, but the sight of the distant horizon and the carnival atmosphere of the amusement park below existed outside Prue's frame of reference. She kept her eyes on the bucket that hovered over her as they went up and dropped below them as they went down.

On the fifth revolution, the keening whine of

Athulak riding the currents overhead cracked Prue's concentration. The spirit's presence alerted her to a danger they hadn't considered. Phoebe hadn't seen what made Jefferson fall or if he was headless when he tumbled. *

Prue fumbled her protection charm out of her pocket as the high-pitched sound intensified and waited eternal seconds for the wheel to start its downward course. At just the right moment, she dropped the leather pouch onto the top of Jefferson's bucket. When it started to slide off, she telekinetically flicked it onto the floor of the car by Jefferson's feet.

Piper's eyes widened as Athulak screamed by the front of their car.

"Don't worry," Prue said, still watching Jefferson's car as they sped past the ground and started upward again. "Your charm should work for both of us."

"I hope you're—" Piper's words were cut off by the grating sound of breaking metal.

Prue and Piper both twisted in their seat. They pulled themselves to their feet so they were braced between the safety bar and the top edge of the bucket canopy. Standing up and facing backward now, Prue looked up and gasped.

The buckets were attached to the wheel on both sides by couplings that swiveled to keep the seats level as the wheel turned. The outer coupling on Jefferson's bucket broke as the ride continued to revolve.

Piper's hands whipped out to cover two directions, freezing the Ferris wheel and everyone watching on the ground below.

Prue quickly assessed the scene. Frozen with his mouth open in terror, the boy was strapped tightly to the car by his seat belt. His hands were clamped on the safety bar.

Jefferson's seat belt had torn loose. Apparently, he had not been holding onto the safety bar when the coupling broke, and he had already started to slide under it. When Piper's freeze ended and the wheel started moving again, he would fall through the struts to his death on the pavement seventy feet below.

"I hope you know what to do," Piper said, "because this hold isn't going to last much longer."

"Understood." Prue breathed in and raised her hands, hoping she had guessed right about what to expect. Once time resumed, the normally horizontal bucket would be hanging vertically by one coupling. She would have only a few seconds to act before the candidate's dangling bucket was carried over the top. She would not have a clear shot to use her power on the way back down.

When time kicked back in, Paul's scream cut through the calliope music, the groan of machinery, and the stunned hush that had settled over the crowd.

Jefferson grabbed for the safety bar, his hands flailing as the bucket swung down into a vertical position. Focused on the candidate, Prue caught him with the force of her telekinetic energies and held him in place before he slipped completely under the safety bar.

Still strapped in by his seat belt, Paul clung to the safety bar when gravity shifted his body. The boy was no longer sitting, but hanging by the strap secured around his waist.

Jefferson's side of the bucket seat had become the bottom when the bucket dropped. The back of the seat and the extension where riders usually rested their feet now formed the sides.

Sweat broke out on Prue's forehead as she shoved the surprised man onto the new bottom of the upright bucket. She continued to hold him as the wheel sped toward the apex of the wheel's circular motion.

"Grab onto the damn bar," Piper muttered.

Prue's heart thudded in her ears as Jefferson grabbed onto the bar with his right hand, pulled up his left knee, and braced his left foot against the curved, metal foot extension. The boy's behind now rested on Jefferson's head. His legs hung down over the man's shoulders and chest. Jefferson used his free hand to steady the screaming child.

With her power still flowing through outstretched hands, Prue caught the candidate's eye as the wheel carried him toward the top. Their gazes locked for a few eternal seconds in which Prue willed Jefferson to hang on. She saw his grip tighten on the bar and Paul's leg before the dangling bucket rounded the apex of the circle and moved Jefferson out of sight and beyond her control.

A shrill wind whistled through the framework of the wheel as Prue and Piper slipped back into their seat. Prue leaned over the safety bar, holding her

breath as she looked down. What used to be Paul's
side of the seat was now the top. It blocked her
view except for one of Paul's legs and Jefferson's
braced foot. As the wheel slowed down and came to
a grinding halt, the boy stopped screaming.

"Well, that was interesting," Piper said. The
bucket rocked as she settled back to wait while the
bodyguards and a park emergency crew rushed to
remove Noel Jefferson and Paul from the swinging
bucket underneath.

Prue slumped, then tensed when she heard the
whistle of Athulak's cry sweeping in from above.

"What's that?" Piper frowned as Prue gripped
her hand.

"Hang on." Prue clung to Piper, relying on the
power of the charm in Piper's pocket to protect
both of them from Athulak's cutting wrath. She
realized that they had been so engrossed with saving Jefferson, they hadn't given any thought as to
whether the vengeful wind spirit would be an
ongoing threat to them.

As the piercing sound closed in, Prue shut her
eyes. Her hair flew wildly in the air churned up by
Athulak's tempestuous approach. A short cry
escaped her as a puff of bitter cold caressed her
cheek.

Then all was still.

CHAPTER
14

Phoebe had seen everything as she slowly wound her way around the kiddie rides and games toward the Ferris wheel. Once she had regained enough strength to walk, she had not been willing to sit and wait. It would take more than a throbbing headache and stomach cramps to keep her away from her sisters during a crisis. They never knew when the Power of Three might be needed.

Apparently, it hadn't been needed this time. Phoebe paused as the hanging bucket seat with Noel Jefferson and Paul came to a stop a few feet off the ground.

Wary of getting too close to anyone, Phoebe walked around the edge of the crowd that had gathered to watch the drama unfold. Flashes went off and cameras whirred as the news teams attached to Jefferson used every available second to record the remarkable story. Phoebe grinned, imagining the evening lead on all the news channels.

"Congressional candidate saves himself and boy from death dive." Every TV report and newspaper would carry a variation of the same theme. It was the top story, Phoebe realized, even though no one would ever know what had really transpired high on the Ferris wheel.

A camera operator bolted from the crowd, hitting Phoebe in the shoulder as he flew by.

"Pardon me!" he yelled, but he kept on running.

Trying to beat the competition to the punch, Phoebe thought. Too bad she didn't have time to tell him there was nothing awful in his immediate future. It had been pure luck that the man hadn't triggered a vision. To avoid any more encounters, she eased into a clear spot between the entrance and the exit for the ride.

Standing on tiptoe, Phoebe waved at Piper and Prue, but they had their eyes closed and didn't see her. She wasn't surprised they were shaken. Standing backward in a swinging Ferris wheel seat seventy feet off the ground would rattle anyone's nerves, even a witch's.

As soon as Jefferson was on solid ground and Paul was in his mother's arms, a maintenance team went to work on the damaged bucket. When the bolts were loosened, they'd drop the bucket and push it aside so the operator could unload the rest of his passengers. It would probably be a few minutes before Piper and Prue could get off.

Several park cops helped Jefferson's two security

guards move the crowd back so the paramedics and the lucky survivors could get out without being crushed in the crowd.

Watching Jefferson's guards, Phoebe was reminded of just how lucky she had been the night before. She had lain awake worrying that they might not be with their boss when disaster struck, and she had been right. The quirks of fate had worked in her and Noel Jefferson's favor this time, but relying on secondhand visions was a mistake she would never make again.

When the wheel moved, Phoebe stepped closer so Piper and Prue would see her when they emerged. Jefferson waved off the paramedics as he walked down the entrance ramp, and the woman refused to relinquish her son. The uniformed medics pointed toward their emergency vehicle. Paul's mom nodded, but she stayed with Jefferson. The boy rested his head on her shoulder with his arms and legs wrapped around her.

The candidate looked shaken, but he was in total control of himself and the situation. The press and the public would eat up the hero angle. Although Noel Jefferson deserved to represent the district on merit, his daring feat on the Ferris wheel had probably just won him the election.

The woman paused when she came abreast of Phoebe. "Hello! I'm so glad you've recovered from your little run-in with Paul." She shifted her right arm to support him and brushed back her hair with her left hand. Then she touched Phoebe's arm.

Phoebe flinched and braced herself, but the vision she expected didn't come.

"I was so worried," the woman went on, "but your sister seemed to know what she was doing."

"Prue is very competent." Phoebe smiled, impressed that the woman cared enough to mention the incident, especially since her son had just had such a harrowing experience. It was easy to understand why Jefferson liked her. She'd make the perfect politician's wife.

Realizing the woman had stopped, Jefferson turned back with a nod and a smile at Phoebe. Every vote counts, Phoebe thought, amused. She was taken by surprise when Jefferson touched her arm. "Lenore told me what happened."

Phoebe swayed as an image of San Francisco, bathed in sunshine under a blue sky and seen from afar, swept through her mind. It wasn't like a normal vision or even those that had plagued her since Athulak had granted her wish. It was a precious glimpse of tomorrow, a fleeting gift that erased the horrors she had absorbed from Stephen Tremaine.

And if she was lucky, Phoebe thought, it was the last unusual vision she would have compliments of Athulak. She hadn't experienced any premonitions when the reporter and Lenore had touched her. Still, that wasn't proof the wish Athulak had granted had been nullified. She wouldn't have a vision if nothing awful loomed in Lenore's and the reporter's futures, either.

"Excuse me, ma'am." The ride operator gripped

Phoebe's shoulders and eased her aside so he could get to his controls.

Phoebe's hopes rose when no images about the ride operator flooded her mind.

"Are you certain you're okay?" Jefferson asked, frowning. "No bumps on the head or anything?"

"I've never felt better, thanks." Overcome with emotion, Phoebe quickly changed the subject. She couldn't explain that his survival had prevented San Francisco from being blown off the map in a future that no longer existed—or that her ability to see that future seemed to be back to normal. "How's Paul doing? That must have been pretty scary up there, huh? But you were so brave."

Paul smiled shyly.

"He'll be fine." The woman hugged the boy a little tighter. "He still wants a doughnut."

"The VIP tent has really good doughnuts," Phoebe said. "I had three!"

Paul giggled.

Jefferson gently rubbed the boy's back. "Can you eat three, Paul?"

"Yep, but I don't want any more Ferris wheel rides, Uncle Noel."

"Now, there's a campaign promise I can make and keep." Jefferson laughed.

Phoebe cocked her head, curious. "Uncle Noel?"

Jefferson nodded and slipped his arm around the woman. "This is my sister, Lenore."

"Really?" Phoebe nodded, then pointed toward the gate as Piper and Prue dashed through and ran over to join them. "These are my sisters, Piper—"

Piper extended her hand. "Hey, there."

"Hello, Piper." Jefferson shook Piper's hand, but his eyes were on Prue. The electrifying chemistry that crackled between them was tangible. When the mustache and his lean, mean partner stepped forward to intervene, the candidate waved them away.

"—and Prue. Professional photographer, single, and free for the rest of the afternoon." Phoebe felt like her old mischievous self when Prue flushed with embarrassment, but she didn't feel bad. Prue was too stuffy to make a move on her own, and Jefferson was obviously hooked. Even better, Phoebe realized. Her headache was fading, and she hardly noticed the gurgle in her stomach.

"Mr. Jefferson, I'm afraid my sister—" Prue hesitated as Jefferson clasped her hand in both of his. "—is, uh, still a bit addled from the heat."

"You kept me from falling." Jefferson continued to stare into Prue's startled eyes.

"No, I—" Prue flashed a wide-eyed glance at Phoebe, but Phoebe was too stunned to respond.

"No, really," Jefferson said. "I know it sounds strange, but it felt as if you were giving me the will and the strength to hang on." Aware that everyone was staring at him, Jefferson cleared his throat. "And I, uh, could use some new head shots."

Prue nodded. "We can probably work something out."

"We should talk about it over lunch," Jefferson said. As he led her away with Lenore and Paul, Prue looked back over her shoulder and zinged the two security men bringing up the rear with a smug smile.

Piper watched them for a moment, then turned to Phoebe with a sad, wistful sigh. "Don't you just love happy endings."

"Yep, but since Noel *is* going to be elected, it won't get too serious. I don't think Prue wants to move to Washington, D.C." Phoebe's eyes widened, and she struggled to keep a straight face when she saw Leo emerge from the crowd behind Piper. He held his finger up to his mouth.

"She certainly doesn't fit the profile of the sweet, unassuming political wife." Piper squealed when Leo covered her eyes with his hands. Before he could get out a "guess who," she jabbed him in the stomach with her elbow.

Phoebe winced as the White Lighter grunted and grimaced. "Hi, Leo," she said.

"Leo!" Mortified and thrilled, Piper covered her mouth and stared as Leo straightened up, still clutching his stomach. Regaining her wits, she immediately launched into a typical Piper-style tirade. "Darn it, Leo! I didn't know it was—"

Without a word, Leo placed his hands on Piper's face and kissed her.

"—you." Eyes brimming with joy, Piper threw her arms around Leo's neck and hugged him. After a moment, she released him, stepped back, and eyed him sternly. "How long?"

"They promised me three days, maybe more." Leo hesitated. "Unless there's a planet-wide catastrophe of some kind."

"Not a problem," Piper said as she linked arms. "We already took care of the planet-wide catastrophes for this week."

"Big time," Phoebe added.

"So I heard." Leo smiled at Piper with adoring eyes. "What would you like to do first?"

"First, I want to ride the merry-go-round ten times. After that, we're going back to my booth to make sure Hard Crackers is set up and ready to rock and roll. Then we're going to dance the afternoon away because that's what people do at P3." As Piper ran through her to-do list, Leo's expression segued from anticipation to resignation. "When the bazaar shuts down at eight, then we can go home."

"How many times do you want to ride the carousel?" Leo asked as they strolled away hand in hand.

"Ten. And I'm going to count." Piper stopped suddenly and whirled to face Phoebe. "Tell Rick he can have the rest of the day off. He was just hanging around waiting to see you anyway."

Oh, yeah, Phoebe thought. Rick.

"You're a very strange girl, you know that?" Rick kept his hands in his pockets and his eyes straight ahead as he walked beside Phoebe toward the stage pavilion.

"You think so?" Phoebe asked, her eyes wide and innocent.

"Yeah." Rick nodded, not happy. "This is the first time a girl's ever asked me to go on her date with another guy."

"It's not a typical date," Phoebe said. She was secretly pleased that Rick was so smitten he had agreed to come along. The only reason she had pushed the joke this far was because he took *everything* seriously and she couldn't resist teasing him. Rick was as hot as she remembered and as nice as she had hoped, but his sense of humor lacked a comprehension of satire and subtle sarcasm.

Only half the folding chairs in front of the stage were filled, and no one was sitting in the front row. The old actor was already onstage, telling stories, and Phoebe was thrilled when the audience laughed at one of his jokes.

"Come on. We can sit front row center." Phoebe motioned Rick to follow.

Rick stopped dead. "That's Roy Hansen."

"Who?" Phoebe looked around, then shrugged as she turned back toward the pavilion.

The old man caught her eye and waved as he spoke into the mike. "Hey, there! How's my best girl?"

"Just fine!" Phoebe yelled back.

"You *know* Roy Hansen, too?" Rick threw up his hands in disbelief.

"You mean"—Phoebe gestured toward the stage—"*that* Roy Hansen?"

"There's only one," Rick said. He stared at the old man in awe. "Roy Hansen was the best cowboy stunt man in Hollywood for thirty years until he got trampled by a bucking bronco and broke about a dozen bones. He's had a second career as a bit player, but no one will ever top him on a horse. Absolutely the best."

"You're right about that. He's also my other date." Phoebe smiled and winked.

Rick finally caught on. Taking her arm, he led her to the front row. "Think you can get me an autograph?" he asked as they sat down.

"Probably." Phoebe pressed closer when Rick draped his arm over the back of her chair. "It'll cost you dinner, though."

Although Phoebe couldn't forget the problems her secret life as a witch might bring to a relationship, she couldn't stop enjoying life, either. As Prue had said, when the real Mr. Right came along, nothing else would matter except being together. In the meantime, though, Phoebe intended to have as much fun as possible.

"That's the best deal I've made in a very long time." Rick brushed her ear with his soft lips, sending shivers up Phoebe's spine.

"Hey!" Roy yelled. "No fair making out with the old guy's girl."

Rick raised his hands playing along.

"Thank you. She's a corker, isn't she? Of course, romance at my age can be downright humiliating." Roy winked and patted his chest. "When the old ticker gets beating too fast, my false teeth fall out."

The audience roared.

"Woohoo!" Rick pumped his approval with his fist.

Phoebe laughed out loud, suddenly overwhelmed with relief and delight. Prue was having lunch with a future congressman. Leo had come home to Piper. Athulak was gone, the world was safe, and she had won the hearts of two totally hot men.

Today the Charmed Ones were batting a thousand.

About the Author

DIANA G. GALLAGHER lives in Florida with her husband, Marty Burke; four dogs; four cats; and a cranky parrot. Before becoming a full-time writer, she made her living in a variety of occupations, including hunter seat equitation instructor, folk musician, and fantasy artist. Best known for her hand-colored prints depicting the doglike activities of *Woof: The House Dragon*, she won a Hugo for Best Fan Artist in 1988.

Diana's first science fiction novel, *The Alien Dark*, was published in 1990. Since then she has written forty intermediate reader and teen novels for Pocket Books in several series, including Star Trek for young readers, The Secret World of Alex Mack, Are You Afraid of the Dark?, Salem's Tails, and Sabrina, the Teenage Witch. Her first (adult) Buffy the Vampire Slayer novel, *Obsidian Fate*, appeared in September 1999 and was followed by two additional Buffy novels, *Prime Evil* and *Doomsday Deck*. *Beware What You Wish* is her first novel in the Charmed series.

"We all need to believe that magic exists."
–Phoebe Halliwell, "Trial by Magic"

When Phoebe Halliwell returned to San Francisco to live with her older sisters, Prue and Piper, in Halliwell Manor, she had no idea the turn her life—*all* their lives—would take. Because when Phoebe found the Book of Shadows in the Manor's attic, she learned that she and her sisters were the Charmed Ones, the most powerful witches of all time. Battling demons, warlocks, and other black-magic baddies, Piper and Phoebe lost Prue but discovered their long-lost half-Whitelighter, half-witch sister, Paige Matthews. The Power of Three was reborn.

Look for a new Charmed novel every other month!

Published by Simon & Schuster
® & © 2004 Spelling Television Inc. All Rights Reserved.

"We're the protectors of the innocent.
We're known as the Charmed Ones."

–Phoebe Halliwell, "Something Wicca This Way Comes"

Go behind the scenes of television's sexiest
supernatural thriller with *The Book of Three*, the
only fully authorized companion to the witty,
witchy world of *Charmed*!